THE HOURGLASS NETWORK

ANDRE SOARES

PROCESS
PROTOCOL

If all mankind were to disappear, the world would regenerate back to the rich state of equilibrium that existed ten thousand years ago. If insects were to vanish, the environment would collapse into chaos.

- E. O. Wilson, "the father of biodiversity"

CONTENTS

1. The Death Bird   1
2. Let There Be Life   3
3. The Killing Shadow   17
4. Baba   25
5. Red Zone. Green Light   29
6. Shh. Mother Nature Came to Collect   37
7. Entropy   43
8. Analog Stage   49
9. The Plagues of Kabul   55
10. A Three-Vector   59
11. The Eye of Ramza   71
12. 1980. 100000   77
13. Out West   91
14. Wolves in Sheep's Clothing   95
15. Like Sands Through the Hourglass   101
16. Sleeper Cells. Agent of Influence   105
17. Which Hand?   111
18. Blackboard Jungle   121
19. The One You Must Not Speak Of   127
20. She Who Had Mastered the Sun   131
21. La Ville Lumière   143
22. Overview Effect   147
23. Shattered Segments   153
24. Rider-Waite: The Magician   161
25. The Arden   167
26. You Shall Love Peace as a Means to New Wars   171
27. Round The Pigs   177
28. Flight   185
29. A Life-Giving Death   191
30. Foreign Agent   195

31. A Throne of Snakes   199
32. He Who Had Mastered the Night   209
33. The Horseman   215
34. The Heir   217
    Epilogue: 221

    Arc Readers Q&A   223
    Afterword   227
    By the Same Author   229

THE DEATH BIRD

AS SHE TEETERED ON THE EDGE OF EXTINCTION...

"*B*aba, *the death bird!*"

Her tiny fingers stretched to the dark skies as a hellfire missile sliced through the night.

The impact *leveled* the village, bodies set ablaze in a court of flames. The child faced a new world, blood strings raining down before her brown eyes. Her father figure, a tall shadow with a rough grip and a bushy beard—her *Baba*—was rushing to reach a man-made hole in the ground, a few feet away; as the child sought refuge in his embrace, her battered skin came in contact with the Kevlar of his bulletproof vest. It felt hot to the touch, metal shrapnel lodged in the fabric like the raised features of a map. The tungsten seared her flesh, drawing red lines on the cream canvas that was her delicate face.

She repressed a scream. To her left, her peripheral vision caught the outlines of corpses, shapes arranged like slabs of meat in a slaughterhouse.

And soon came the darkness. The oppressive hold of an underground cave.

There were carvings on the bedrock. Torchlights sought her

hazel eyes. Some elderly figures with crooked frames had converged toward them.

"Ahriman's influence. The work of shapeshifters!"

"The Americans. They got the wrong target!"

"No, *Agda*. Your clan brought a blood curse. Death dealer!"

A fight ensued somewhere in the child's vicinity, as a serrated blade pierced the fabric of a robe and produced a distinct sound she recognized. The fools were like human-sized rats that had begun gnawing at each other, both literally and figuratively. While rushing to a diverging path, *Baba* waved the knives away, skillful and elegant in his stance.

Death was outpaced by the two escapees, left to argue with drug kingpins and warlords who drank the blood of their casualties and chewed on their sawed bones, manic laughter growing feebler in the distance.

Further ahead, *Baba* found an eerie quiet plane, disrupted only by the occasional water drops falling from the fractured foundations above.

"*Shh*, Malia. We might live tonight."

2

LET THERE BE LIFE

KABUL. MARCH 21, 2025.

S heer curtains swayed under the light breeze of a warm spring. A dancing shadow haunted its waving curves, progressing along a high wall.

The target was breathing heavily, tucked in luxurious sheets of grade A Mulberry silk. Here, opulence was an explicit statement, delivered through solid gold desks and sisal grasscloth wallpapers that suggested a particular inclination to the showcasing of obnoxious wealth.

I am a sheep, but I growl like a wolf.

The killer's face was concealed behind a breathing device coated in ceramic plates, its flesh tightening with each motion. His handgun's silencer embraced the angular lines of a platform bed and found the soon-to-be-dead civilian, oblivious to the intrusion, nested in a comforting dreamworld.

The mysterious killer bridged the gap between the target and his own, quiet shadow: a shot rang, muffled and snappy. The target's forehead sustained a deadly wound, his face forever frozen in discomfort.

10. 9. 8. 7. 6. 5.

5.

A few miles away, the quiet *hum* of a radioactive diamond battery crossed the U.S. embassy's heavily fortified gates. The state-of-the-art electric truck swept the welcome committee with its directional headlights and parked before a tall concrete structure that flaunted an exacerbated brutalist architecture; its sharp angles bloomed outward like an invasive weed, offering a stark contrast with the natural gardens that neighbored its fenced limits. The vehicle's driver's sharp, blue eyes sought the skies through the windshield, his blonde strands shining under the moonlight. Soldiers gathered around the truck as it quietly shut down.

"Mr. Keller, deputy chief of mission. Welcome home," a muffled voice delivered from across the windows' ballistic glass.

The driver stepped out of the vehicle and shook hands. He replied, "Thank you, Alston. Had a pleasant trip. Kabul is such a... Cultural powerhouse. The closest we'll ever get to a Garden of Eden, if you ask me. Magnificent. Radiant."

The soldiers approved in a polite nod, neutral in their facial expressions.

Alston replied, "Indeed. One of the cradles of civilization."

All parties present nodded in quiet agreement once more. Keller, the blue-eyed driver and high-ranking diplomat, was issued a breathing mask, light and plated in black ceramic. The soldiers followed suit and donned their own chemical gas masks, shielded from the loud source of a nearby celebration by the tall structure that towered over them like a paternal figure.

Personnel from the embassy and local officials were praising the ratification of a historic treaty with the Afghan government in a loud, joyful noise close by. Beyond the razor-sharp edges of the concrete block, string lights ran from numerous banners whose letters formed *Kabul Treaty.* 5th

Energy Symposium. Smoky meats, spices and Afghan folk songs entertained the crowds that were spread evenly across a manicured lawn, one that edged to breathtaking views of the city.

Deputy chief of mission Keller was known to be a quiet man, a creature of habit, but also a field diplomat. He gauged the soldiers who faced his truck's hood, his sharp German features then shifting to the starry night skies.

For a fleeting instant, time ran its course peacefully.

Boom.

A blinding blast consumed the compound, casting the grounds in strobing flashes of artificial UV light.

The sonic boom rippled through the city, reaching south to a chaotic bazaar fragranced with layered spices and thick full grain leathers.

The flash-like fulmination found no resistance. Terrorism was a ghost of the past, a distant recollection for the younger Afghan population, residents of a utopia blending tradition and cutting-edge innovations.

Faces froze, searching for an answer in the northern hills, where the detonation originated. There was no smoke, no flames, no apparent structural damage, leaving the crowds to wonder, fueling the emergence of overlapping conversations.

A truck carved a path into the market's center, screeching to a halt as it reached an old fountain. The streetlights perched above the bazaar's ceiling drapes spotlighted the features of a young woman, her feet firmly planted onto the truck's bed. Her hazel eyes competed with scar tissue from apparent lacerations that ran across her face, like the scribbles of a madman. Her silky hair shone in a bun, raising the seriousness of her otherwise juvenile features.

She brought fear to the bystanders' eyes, superseding the flameless explosion heard from afar.

They knew her. The legends spoke of a devil matching her description.

"Scared sheep, like a shifty flock," she yelled, commanding their attention. Two men stepped out of the truck, armed to the teeth. They were older, rugged and intentional: the product of another era, the last of a dying breed.

"What happened to the proud horsemen running the valleys? The warriors whose sovereignty was never disputed nor questioned? You all live like roaches, SCATTERING when your masters enter the room and flip the switch *on*."

She jumped off the truck's bed and spat on the dusty floor.

"What a shame. *Ai bozdilha!*"

Black pouches were laid out on the vehicle's cargo bed, as well as a cylindric device coated in matte black.

The mercurial woman resumed, "You will be given a choice tonight. Follow the ruthless prophet of a new world. Or die the subject of pain." The two henchmen climbed the bed with ease. She approached the stunned crowd, and crouched before a child, a daughter who reminded her of this little girl, the one bathed in blood, shielded from a drone strike by a benevolent father figure.

"Do you want to live?" she asked the small child. The latter's eyes sought her mother's.

But they were frozen in fear, unable to offer comfort or closure.

The self-appointed prophet stood and grabbed the mother's throat, crushing her windpipe with an iron grip; the sound of crackling sparks preceded her collapse, as life vacated her shell. The henchmen issued warning shots, advising against any move on their leader. The child ran to her mother, a soulless corpse lying crooked in the dirt.

The *prophet* spoke again. "Child, do you want to live?" The little girl fought heavy tears, repressed by sporadic tremors, and turned around. She nodded in agreement.

The self-proclaimed envoy of God addressed the crowd once more, satisfied with her decision.

"For those of you scholars and elders, you've heard the stories. I killed and birthed killers. All the same." She paused and looked at her wristwatch. "You have thirty seconds to redeem yourselves. We have twenty breathing devices here, a countermeasure to what's coming next. Those who decide to use them will serve me. The others will die a painful death. Disorderly conduct or bold objections to my rule will be met by death, also."

The bystanders panicked. They heard of and read on the warlord, known to overdeliver on her promises. The tales of the Wakhan corridor's heiress seeded fear in their malleable minds, haunting the collective memory like visions of horror. Western powers were no match for her ruthlessness, they thought.

Most lined up in a file, tuned in to their sense of self-preservation, unwilling to die, yet afraid to sell their soul. As the breathing devices' stock depleted, Malia jumped back on the truck's bed, light and soundless.

"Move back!"

Some of the braver souls had fled through nearby arteries; they feared Allah more than the death bringer and refused to consider serving the unhinged monster that was caged within her.

She turned to one of the henchmen, an elder radiating in timeless strength.

"*Baba*, ready?"

"Yes, Malia. We live tonight."

The cylindrical device mounted on the flatbed sung a melodious chime; it shot upward in a flawless vertical and breached the night vault. Another flameless blast roared through the city's center. UV lights bounced off an invisible dome shielding Malia's vehicle.

Oh.

The nearby buildings crumbled, as artificial compounds and inorganic matter were converted to living *things*, directed by the blasting cracks of wild roots shooting from the ground at light speed. Soon, the bazaar shapeshifted into a riotous jungle, overgrown vegetation reemerging from the ashes of a terrifying vacuum.

Baba and his mysterious associate rushed to the truck's cabin as Malia watched her fellow countrymen and women disperse like rats in a London flood. Tears welled up in her faded brown eyes but there was no emotion conveyed, rather simply a bland flesh composite sweating the cries of an upcoming war. She struck the cabin twice before they forced a path through the newly grown canopy.

Kabul was changing before her eyes.

She was a goddess meddling with her creation, interfering with the modern world, with its presumed trajectory. Alongside her northbound itinerary, bodies collapsed, twisted in pain, eyes like white marbles housed in green sarcophagi. Structures transmuted into trees, shrubs, parterres, mosses and floral compositions swirling to visions of delirious dreams.

The atmosphere felt *heavier*; billions of invisible needles gently stretched Malia's brown skin. A river flowing alongside the dirt road she traveled on appeared, revealing a full moon dancing on its aggrieved current. Swarms of locusts sang in the dark, falling shortly after takeoff, outlived by Turkistan roaches flapping their wings in a desperate pledge.

Malia watched the disease spread with fulfillment; this new world was foreign to her yet felt more legitimate, like it had assumed its true form after gestating in the toxicity of an unbalanced placenta. She checked her watch and struck the cabin's roof; the vehicle sped up, breaching through a maze of serpentines flanked by clay homes.

Her heart raced, shattering the barrier that held back a surge of maddening anticipation; a presence was felt—the missing piece on her handcrafted chessboard.

"*Baba*, second on the left, red gates!" Malia shouted over the rising winds.

The vehicle slowed to a stop.

To their left, a remarkably tall frame guarded the gate, his piercing, glowing eyes fixed on the truck as it came to a shuddering halt. His shaved scalp displayed streaks carved into its flesh like Martian landscapes. His jawline was enclosed in small ceramic plates, which also obstructed his nose bridge and mouth contours.

The Mulberry silk's assassin.

Malia, still perched on the flatbed, clapped once.

"*Agda!*" she ordered. The giant answered the call like a trained dog and leaped on the truck's bed, its suspensions bending under the strain.

"We have twenty-five minutes to reclaim what is ours. You will kill," shared Malia as the white pickup resumed its course on an uphill road leading to a massive villa.

Dust rose in the night. Other trucks joined the lead vehicle, pieces reclaimed from small neighboring arteries. Malia and the merchant of death snapped open a compartment attached to the bed's gate; they found bulletproof vests, rifles and two tactical backpacks. The remainder of the convoy followed suit and geared up in an unspoken promise.

A sea of metals raced toward the higher levels of a tortuous path. Malia looked up and spotted a condensation trail in the magical skies.

Baba, she thought. *We are the death birds now.*

The trucks reached the end of the road. Malia and the

hitman she called *Agda* dismounted, leading the charge against the objective, a compound that drew its outlines across a veil of dust.

A blonde-haired man with glacial blue eyes, his pale complexion brushed with strokes of a dying tan, was at the gates, reviewing the structure ahead, a fortified villa whose strong Islamic influences delivered a live action *Arabian nights.* A colorful garden showcased its many extensions, emergent layers that towered above the gated perimeter Malia's army was now occupying.

"Keller, how was the social function?" she asked.

The man turned to her and bowed. "Well. You won't have to worry about foreign interference, besides mine. The other embassies have been shut down. It seems we're on schedule."

He smiled.

"Great. It's a few things in there. Goods stolen from the Durrani. From my ancestors."

Keller politely nodded, "Naturally," and waved a hand.

Inside the compound, voices began rising from the giant fortress.

"Hurry! Something at the gate!"

"Hey!"

Keller's soldiers, the men who had welcomed him to the U.S. embassy, had already spread alongside the earth-toned ramparts, their weapons trained high above the walls, barrels equipped with elevation sights shaped like rectangles.

Their muzzles found the building from which the objections to their invasion originated. Triggers squeezed and smoke grenades launched above the garden's canopy.

Glass shattered. *Thumps* bounced off in the night. Columns of smoke rose from inside the courtyard, dancing in tango with the winds.

The dream turned into the product of nightmares. Malia

approached the red iron gate guarding a path to a majestic Moorish door of recursive crescent-shaped patterns.

Nearby, AK-47s drew sharper, menacing and bullish. She retrieved a small metal plate from her armored vest and stuck it on the gate's locking mechanism.

"Clear?"

"Clear!"

She and *Agda* moved aside, as she pressed a wireless detonator cradled into her hand. The gate blew outward. Across from her position, Keller nodded, calm and collected.

Malia turned to her right hand and ordered, "Go, *Agda*. Kill."

She followed his agile frame into the courtyard, leaving *Baba* to trail behind. The masked shadow began lining shots, the barrel of his rifle foreshadowing his footwork.

In the dense smoke, bodies collapsed, the sound of their fall replicated like ripples on a pond. Keller followed, indulging in the madness.

Malia approached the villa's opulent entrance with her mute bodyguard and stuck another explosive charge in between both door panels. "Breaching," she signaled.

Keller and his group stepped back, checking the building's upper decks. He fired blindly at the windows, shattering glass and frames in a dramatic performance.

"OUT, ROACHES!" His voice was a clamant statement, a charge forcefully penetrating the smokes.

Malia's charge detonated, the deafening sound reigning over Keller's gunshots.

Agda entered first; his terrifying frame launched against the door panels.

Inside, an obscene amount of wealth obstructed the path to more grounded wants. Luxurious arabesque tiles were paired with a central water fountain that featured complex geometric mosaics made of imperial porcelain. Massive olive trees were arranged in symmetrical rows, ancient and twisted.

Malia placed a hand on Agda's chest, while Keller and his group stormed the upper levels.

"You will guard the perimeter while I break in," she ordered the silent golem.

He tilted his head in agreement, his eyes fixed onto her. She walked the courtyard and ran a finger through the fountain's surface as she passed by, drawing an ephemeral trail in the water. Her eyes found her own wavy reflection; it gave the illusion of another *invisible man*'s rendition, parts of her facial features erased by the troubled source.

"Down!" Keller's diplomatic ways transformed upstairs.

Malia looked up. In the hallway above, civilians in robes were lying on their stomachs, their fingers interlocked above their head.

She addressed Keller from downstairs. "Good, line those fat rats up! Thieves!" she yelled, as she approached a steel door with a flat handle, one that disrupted the far wall's mesmerizing Islamic calligraphy.

An emitting diode flashed a red light above the handle. Malia took her backpack off and opened the front pouch, laughing at some strange prospect she seemed to be reminiscing.

I. 2.

She retrieved three squared blocks of a dark olive-green compound, pasty in texture and warm to the touch.

May you grant me passage.

Her hands also found a wire connecting three pill-sized metal probes to a small switch. Finally, she searched the bag for another switch.

As she began inserting the pill-sized probes into the pasty blocks, she stole a glance at the upper level to her right and raised her voice.

"You know, Keller, this is the issue. *Baba* will tell you. This... overreliance on technological assets. The rewiring of our brains as we... looking? For assistance instead of... leading the charge."

She placed the blocks around the door handle, arranged them in a triangular pattern and flipped the wired switch that connected to the charges *on*. A few steps back allowed her to find cover behind the fountain's base, her agile hands expertly unrolling the wire.

"We've become so far removed from our natural habitat, our primal functions. We want to control the things that live among us. It's no longer a collaborative effort. Even those who claim they never were slave masters or slave runners... they are, in some form. I am too, Keller. But I work for Mother Nature now. *Baba*?"

Keller seemed amused by the eloquent monologue, smiling from the upper deck. Malia connected the wire to her own detonator.

"Yes, Malia?" a voice replied from one of the rooms above.

"I'm breaching."

Footsteps echoed above, as *Baba*'s tall, dignified frame returned to Malia in haste.

"Ok, *gulaaba*." She smiled at the term of endearment and flipped her own switch.

The explosive charges detonated in a sequence, from top to bottom, and produced three metallic *clangs* that traveled the space. The door swung open, light and lifeless.

Malia, *Baba* and Agda entered, engaging with a stairwell that precipitated them into a down spiral. Ahead, the dancing lights of wooden torches cast small shadows on the stone walls.

More mercenaries had joined the parade as Malia reached a basement that housed wonders encased in glass boxes.

The space felt magical, or of spiritual significance. Horsemen and angels were carved onto the stone walls, shooting upward from the uneven edges of a dirt floor. Items were showcased throughout the space, their description etched onto golden plaques mounted on small pillars. The swaying flames of the torches highlighted various details as they burned a warm fire.

Baba grabbed Malia and held her in a fatherly embrace. *Agda* returned to the bottom of the stairs, his rifle aimed at their upward sprawling.

"This is ours, Malia," *Baba* struggled. "The Durrani's... our bloodline. Powerful rulers with no inclination to give in to the colonizers' demands. Or the snakes within our very own ranks. *Yes!*"

Malia gave him a squeeze and approached the items. There were bangles, sculptures, tapestry, traditional robes woven into intricate patterns, ancient texts from philosophers and prophetic figures. Her eyes swept the secret exhibit, wowed at the opportunity to reconstruct the shattered portions of her traumatizing history.

I would belong, once more. No more of the rapists' lustful eyes, or the murderers' touch.

Seismic motions brought her back to reality. She walked to a piece whose coarse fabric shone from subtle gold accents imprinted into the fiber. *Baba* approached.

"Allah, Malia. The supreme creator's. It is yours to claim."

Malia asked, "Rightfully so?"

He nodded. "The sheer scope of your intervention. Reshaping this world. Yes."

They both came to a silent agreement and retrieved brick hammers from their backpacks. Malia clapped her hands twice. Agda sought her commanding eyes as he stepped closer.

"*Agda*, go signal Keller we need transport." The quiet killer bowed and flew through the stairwell.

Glass shattered under the repeated assault of fine cracks.

The noise reverberated against the space's boundaries, feeding off Malia and *Baba*'s determination, off their unwavering conviction.

They were mindful not to break the casings atop the artifacts or drive their hammer too far in. Footsteps grew louder. Agda and a few men had arrived, small bags in hand.

Malia and *Baba* stopped. She ordered, "Take it all. One scratch and I will press against your throat with my bare hands until life no longer *inhabits* you."

The men bowed and started packing the treasures with caution. Malia returned to the exposed cloak she was seeking and grabbed it, feeling on the fabric and kissing its edges.

She looked around for a brief moment, reminiscing of the caves she grew up in, the den of wolves, driven to hiding by the Americans, the tight-skinned pigs who tried to leverage her land, and capitalize on her culture. But her resentment existed beyond expected quarrels with the West; some of her own people had subjected her to a mind-numbing pain.

She allowed herself to channel one of the visions she had compartmentalized. An old man with a drooping nose showed rotten teeth, his eyes gleaming of excitement as he moved on her, the pliers he held pressing on something in between her legs.

Flashes of a searing pain had paralyzed her body at the time, as she had tried to understand what enticed the older man...

Fortunately, he had failed to mutilate her, though his sadistic nature left scars no one knew of.

Baba had stepped up early on and rescued her. He offered a more stable environment, gave her the opportunity to *exist*, and grow into the feared warrior she was today.

She thought of the surface, entire structures brought down by the hand of a new god, the emergence of a new disease.

Let there be life, she thought.

3

THE KILLING SHADOW

TWO HOURS AND THIRTY MINUTES EARLIER – KABUL

Durrani. Baba. They travel by horse. Rejecting most modern technology besides weaponry and chemicals. Use of child labor. Patriarchal subset. Little to no oversight into the reinvesting of drug trafficking proceeds.

"Feed is on."

A voice brushed the many equations juggled with, deep within the man's sharp mind. He was calm, collected, yet commanding. His use of personal space suggested efficiency. The slight rightward lean made effective use of the door's padding in the event of a rollover. A center console allowed his unit to visualize the drone feed all at once. An HK45 handgun was holstered on his right hip and a LVOA-C rifle rested by his right leg. He had considered three hundred and seventy-six scenarios in this pursuit, as his driver sped through the narrow streets of the Taimani Project, a vibrant neighborhood known for its art scene and bustling night life.

Man plans—fate laughs.

The Taliban had withdrawn from Kabul after a successful string of assets freeze conducted by financial forensics at the CIA. They left the city's brilliant and resilient womanhood in charge of many districts, including this one.

The men in this unmarked Toyota truck were also part of the intelligence agency yet had more lethal inclinations.

The drone feed appeared on the display unit mounted onto the dashboard. A black and white screen displayed a group of horsemen meeting by the bank of a wide river. There were unidentified boxes lined up by the embankment.

"Thermal, please."

To the right of the screen, numbers fluctuated as the drone stationed over the targets, unseen. The sun had set, but the thermal imagery was crystal clear, drawing the suspects in shades of orange and blue.

The leader grabbed a pen and motioned circles around the boxes, tapping on the screen. "Can we identify those containers, Control?"

A voice echoed through his earpiece, "Negative. No HUMINT on the contents. Do you believe there's a hazard?"

He stared into the feed, brows raised. The horsemen were still, unsuspecting.

"By the Helmand, yes, possibly. But there's no other collateral nearby. We'll sweep the site for pollutants and radioactive matter in phase two. You may proceed. Stay on target."

"R1, this is Control. Good copy. Out."

The truck screeched to a halt, tires slicing through the darkness of a back alley. The ghosts of old warehouses haunted the abandoned industrial area.

The mysterious man's chest was constricted by an oppressive, invisible hand.

4-2-6 breathing. Inhale. Hold. Exhale.

The methodical killer addressed his pack, suffering in the utmost secrecy. Rifles found their rightful owners and postures straightened in the modified truck.

"Northeast block. I count on your discretion. HUMINT mentioned ten girls, but couriers are infamously unreliable in this region. See *Geronimo.* You will count your kills and stack on me. We need a small signature and a quick exfil. Gear?"

"Check 1."

"Check 2."

"Check 3."

"Check 4."

The men blended well with the local population, boasting golden-hued skin undertones, sharp features, thick black hair and flawless Dari speech. But their exchange in the truck told another story, one that may involve culturally sensible foreigners, rather.

The truck's doors opened to an instant blackout spanning over five blocks, one the driver had purposely caused. Darkness settled in, meeting no objection in this abandoned area.

The men swarmed a small courtyard to their right, rushing to heavy coiling doors that concealed a massive space. The op leader struck the coiling doors twice, generating waves dancing on the shiny metal. He said, "*Qatra qatra darya maisha.*"

The rolling doors shot upward, loud with a painful shriek. *Tsik.*

The leader's rifle shot the doorman's legs while the others pushed the fire-rated curtain up. Another round found the man's head, as he met the concrete floor.

"R1. One kill."

In the span of seconds, they were all inside, positioned behind wide concrete pillars, the coiling doors closing back up.

From the further end, voices inquired, "*Mara?*"

The four-man team advanced in two-man files, inching

closer to their targets. In the coldness of the concrete hideout, they held higher ground, their footwork an ode to the art of war. The leader's eyes gained clarity, spotting four guards struggling in the low-visibility environment.

The four CIA officers quietly shifted into a V-shaped formation and squeezed their triggers. Death rained down on the guards, bodies stacked upon one another, their irregular twitches raking the floor.

"R1. Two kills."

"R2. One kill."

"R3. Two kills."

The lead moved past the dead flesh, unbothered, and found an access point at the far edge of the wide space they had swept clean.

A barn door. Behind, something, or someone was scratching at its sleek metallic surface, irregular and erratic in their ways.

"Āmereyekāyey. Americans," the leader called. The scratching slowed to a stop.

The lead's right-hand man found a set of keys on one of the corpses, anticipating his orders. There was a synergy between the men, like the shared consciousness of a hive. The door unlocked and revealed a vision of horrors.

"What—"

Within the suffocating walls of a ship container, women shared an IV circuit, rocking in rotten chairs under a feeble light. A younger girl had frozen in fear, her bloody nails pulsing against her chest. The air reeked of ammonia and iron.

"Control, I'm transmitting for the mission report, no response needed. They've been drugged. Most likely shipping to the Ramza compound we heard of on the waves. Shared dreams, ideological conditioning and their current stage, the alteration of their vital functions. See the breathing patterns?" The leader pointed at one of the women, her thoracic cage inflating and deflating in a rapid-fire. "It may be reversible. And this young lady was untouched. Or maybe she was, in other unfathomable ways. Let's pray not."

The men searched the container for sensitive intelligence but found nothing of significance. There were no personal effects, no pictures. Foul-smelling buckets had been set in a corner.

The leader resumed, "Control, this is R1 again. Prepare to strike. We have our package."

"Good copy, R1. Standby."

They ripped the IVs from the punctured skins and grabbed the women whose closed eyelids fluttered feverishly. The op leader motioned for the young girl to follow. She looked around and stood, hesitant.

He spoke to her in a proper Dari. "I knew a girl like you. Battered, left for dead, raised by life. I'm offering you a better outcome than hers."

The girl burst in tears, seeking refuge behind the man.

They proceeded to exit the hellish slaughterhouse, carrying the dead weights of the sedated, silent in their movements yet swift.

Outside, a van had pulled up behind their armored truck. The men loaded the women and the little girl in the spacious sprinter and returned to their vehicle as it took off in the night.

The block regained power and light. And serenity.

"Control, this is R1."

Their vehicle seamlessly merged into an expressway, camouflaged in the heavy traffic of night owls, rich partygoers and service workers.

"R1, this is Control. We have authorization per findings."

The drone feed reappeared on the center screen. The lead reviewed the live footage; more horsemen had gathered around the unidentified packages.

"Control, this is R1. Four more tangos? Any other change?"

"Four additional tangos, R1. No further changes."

"Hit i—"

The video feed shut down.

The audio transmission went dark.

A loud explosion roared up north, its booming sound reaching the truck's cabin.

The drone operator's nasal voice resurfaced. "R1, we lost control. Advise?"

The leader motioned for the driver to pull over. He stepped out of the vehicle.

Further ahead, an overpass began collapsing. The patterns were strange, however, like the breathing of the drugged women they had recovered.

This was not the outcome of a demolition drill, or a conventional blast.

A disease.

The leader returned to the vehicle and shouted, "This is R1, we are compromised! Headed to Q5. Going dark."

He looked at his driver and ordered, "Go, go, go!"

The truck struggled a U-turn in the chaotic traffic and crossed the flat median to head southbound. But the disease spread faster, consuming the concrete and metals, civilian commuters quickly engulfed in death.

It soon caught up with the vehicle, as the men raced to the nearest exit. The Toyota's reinforced frame crumbled in fine grains, followed by the weapon systems, comms, and attachments. The leader and his pack fell twenty feet down an avalanche of black sand.

Around them, civilians crashed, their screams silenced by the shifting earth. Necks twisted to rupture. Softer flesh was lacerated.

It was hard to grasp what had just happened, the extent and

nature of the attack, the motives, the methods. All a blur of dark twists.

The CIA officers covered their heads, moving diagonally toward the edges of the landslide, where air pockets subsisted. They swam back up through sheer determination, their breathing slow and steady, the memories of lifetimes a solid thread they held onto.

Before long, the world fell into silence.

BABA

"Some men marvel at God's work, others at the cut of a garment. The latter are foolish, lack insight. They will perish first. The former... well, I am your God now."

Malia addressed armed crowds gathered in the clearing of a rogue jungle. A fog of war rose from the immediate perimeter, shielding the gathering from an outsider's gaze.

Beyond the fog, the sounds of collapsing structures rang duplicated chords that resonated like thunder.

Malia resumed, "Mankind was in dire need of a new God, a new figure of authority. No more blanket statements. No more false equivalence, nor promises. I am the one! I was chosen to make the hard decisions! You will follow me blindly, to the edge of this Earth. You will not question my motives or my methods. You will execute. Again, blindly."

The men and women whose eyes were glued to their leader acquiesced in a subtle nod. Their glossy optics swayed between a wet sadness and a scorching hatred, never quite clearly positioned on the spectrum. They were breathing in rapid gasps, like the phantom choir of an afterlife circus.

Malia raised a hand and dispatched them; the body frames and weapons they carried along vanished in the fog. She turned toward her father figure, standing to her right, and inquired, "*Baba*, I am angry. How will I go about it?"

The elder rubbed his thick beard, his eyes dancing to the beat of a new wilderness.

"What makes you angry, child?"

"Mankind. Why do I have to coerce them into a decision? To pour billions into mass murder and ecoterrorism. It's not remorse, it's not fear I'm feeling. It's frustrations."

Baba briefly glanced at Agda, posted behind Malia, docile and neutral like a gentle giant.

He answered, "We have... limitations. It is wrong to believe that there is anything remotely close to a collective response with humans. Every action, every thought is rooted in individualism. And that drives every reaction, feeds every motive, satisfies all agendas. That is why I grew this empire, *gulaaba*. Why I trained you. We could not afford the luxury to wait for a sensible response to our planet dying, to the arms race. Weak minds sink under prosperity as well as adversity. Make peace with this."

Malia sought comfort in his eyes. What she found was rather a ruthless determination and the hardening nature of past horrors, but no validation of her feelings. Against the backcloth of a fast-growing flora, they headed west toward the outskirts of former Kabul, cutting the verbal exchange short.

Agda followed. He was monitoring the emerald skies as they trekked the *dead zone* their bomb had produced. They were ghosts walking their nation, freed from foreign interference and invasive surveillance.

High above, satellites were drawn into orbit, bursting into ashes like quiet fireworks. Communications with the outside world had ceased, turning all digital footage of Kabul into an ominous black screen. The arid deserts bloomed into fertile soils whose green layers brought a cooler breeze. Water began dripping from hairy stems and complicated surface roots, feeding a parched world that had believed it was on borrowed time. Plastics and pollutants dissolved, freeing real estate for clear streams and luxuriant footpaths.

The scope of the transformation was dizzying, bringing confusion to the general population, as well as the few remaining industrialists who had milked Afghanistan for convertible resources.

Soon, *their* bodies failed to adjust; this Earth presented new guidelines, a new atmospheric composition Malia had imposed on mankind.

Suddenly, *their* flesh was drained of its life.

"Help!"

Weak bones rattled against Malia's ankles, triggering Agda's protective instincts. She raised her hand and stopped him in his tracks. *Baba*'s protégé looked down at the naked shape of a survivor, one gasping for air. His eyes were carved into dark sockets; his lips glowed in a purple hue.

"Hellllll—"

Malia crouched and reached for his throat. She whispered, "Hell was something you helped shape, you and your sheepish peers. This is the ushering of a cleaner slate. Our survival. Now, die brave as you lived a coward."

She paused and studied his response. The young man trembled with fury, chained to the ground by invisible shackles.

"I'll do you a favor, little bird—you won't carry fear into the afterlife."

She crushed his throat with supernatural strength, pressing on the pale tissue, stressing the muscles to their breaking point, shattering his skeletal framework.

The body twitched with faint protests and surrendered to

her might; his soulless eyes told the story of a fallen civilization, one that had failed to predict a future its own practices had fore-shadowed.

5

RED ZONE. GREEN LIGHT

"Red zone. This is green light. How copy?"

The CIA officer clutched a wired phone whose cables were stapled to a rough bedrock. Tremors shook the ceiling, dust particles coughed up by the sickly bodies of men who had escaped a foreign atmosphere above ground. Their garments weren't theirs, sets of mismatched clothing that were ill-fitting.

But their leader had been there before, at the edge of a cliff whose steep side quickly eroded. He learned to favor the bigger picture, the *true* way out.

"Red zone. This is green light. How copy?"

He looked at his men, his face pulled inward by furrowed brows and wrinkles; they were shivering, pacing and counting imaginary steps, or visualizing combat models.

"Rich?"

"Yes boss, feeling great. Confirming we're still headed southbound."

Trapped in a maze of dark tunnels, water biting at their ankles, their only lifeline was an inner voice: one of sharp tone and decisiveness.

The leader checked the wiring running along the tunnel's wall. He tapped it and retwisted the connection to the candlestick phone he clutched, strengthening the red, green, and black wires forming a spiral between the phone's base and the remainder of the cable line.

"Red zone. This is green light. How copy?"

"Green light? You have cleansed your body?"

"Yes. How will you cleanse your soul?"

"Is this a secured line?"

"Yes."

"Qurban?"

"Yes. Ms. Lowes?"

A short pause built tension. The phone operator hesitated.

"Affirmative. Riz, it's good to hear from you. What's your status?"

His men smiled, halting their pacing. Death had knocked on their door, but there was a chance it would vacate the premises before being let in.

"We survived. There's been a couple of explosions about three miles north of the Taimani Projects and maybe fifteen miles northwest, most likely by the embassy row. The perpetrator is unknown. No claim. But it is unprecedented. We found shelter so I had time to process what we saw. It is… terraforming technology, maybe? It consumed buildings and vehicles and *transformed* the air we breathe. We were suffocating above ground. Bodies everywhere. Overgrown vegetation. Something… dystopian. Digital means of communication are no longer viable, also."

"What about the radius? The exposure?"

Riz Qurban briefly glanced at his men, studying their breathing patterns and surveying superficial injuries.

He returned to his conversation. "That's the problem,

ma'am. It's still expanding in mass, like a contagious disease, a cancer. No further symptoms as of now, though."

"Understood. What is your take on that?"

"This is ecoterrorism, minus the usual shortcomings. Whoever did this had a plan. They have resources and political support, possibly. They've been preparing for years most likely. No one saw it coming. And I'm confident this was just an introduction to something much bigger. Or a pilot."

"Okay. Did you manage to exfil the hostages?"

"Yes. But we lost contact with their transport."

A silence settled. The ambient buzz of a crisis response team shot through the candlestick phone. Qurban looked at his men and gauged their condition once more, displaying an unusual interest in their health. But they were formidable warriors, spies, and diplomats. Resilient and patient. Given the fatal injuries sustained by others on the surface, he considered himself fortunate.

"Riz. Where are you located?"

"Prepare to copy."

"Ready."

Qurban took a few seconds to confirm his location. His hands waved a piece of paper against a dying light.

"34.503°N 69., Block 157-158 Walkway, Kabul, Afghanistan. The Babar Garden."

Ms. Lowes was calm. Her voice impenetrable.

"Shuhadah E Saleheen cemetery. Head south, then turn left at the next junction. Continue until you find a service door to your right. There will be Hazmat suits and supplies. And an overhead exit. Provided the area is still untouched, you should be able to find a transport and cross the border to Pakistan."

"Understood. Do we have tactical support east of the border?"

"Yes, one moment."

Above, strong vibrations began fracturing the ceiling. Riz raised a hand and signaled his men to stack on him.

"Ok. Key *Lang 143* when you cross the border. We'll have covers and a transport."

"*Lang 143*. Good copy. On the way. Out."

Qurban let the old analog phone dangle from its thin wiring. He rushed south, his shadow overpowering the feeble lights and wires running along his sides.

The tunnel was an old subway outfit. Through clear waters, beat-up tracks appeared bolted to massive wooden planks divided by floating gravel.

The air was cold and *charged*; it felt like a muffled dream possessed by an intermittent sharpness. Hunger had crept on the men, but they were conditioned to operate under such circumstances. None questioned their leader or argued his furious pacing. There was only one, single common goal: self-preservation.

Miles of a painful trek led to a junction. The right corridor sloped upward to a dark conduit. The left pathway curved right to more flickering lights. The men rushed left, their muscles tensed, their frames slightly bent forward.

Their silence had left room for foreshadowing sounds. Footfall on the tracks, fabric sweeping the walls, shadows intersecting with the path of light... the CIA officers stood for more lethal iterations of Red Riding Hood, walking an underground maze to evade the Big Bad Wolf's disease. However, they had sharper teeth than *she*, and a more cunning mind.

"Here."

Riz opened a fireproof door whose steel shrieked in pain.

This is how it begins.

Beyond the entry frame, Hazmat suits hung on hooks bolted to the bare walls, black crates neatly arranged beneath them. At the far end of the room, a ladder led to a well of light.

The breeze sweeping from above appeared harmless to the agents' lungs.

"Suit up and load up on supplies," Riz ordered. He scanned the laddered exit and searched the blue skies for strange anomalies. There were none.

"How are we moving, boss?" one of the men asked as he drank from a glass bottle whose cap seal he had checked.

Riz remained silent for a few seconds, waiting for his men to suit up, seeking a flaw in their outfitting. As they stocked up on dried foods and liquids, he answered, "Compact. Small visual signature. Light weaponry, if the conditions permit it. We need to blend in. There's most likely displacement happening. Refugee routes. An exodus. And I know this region well."

He paused to inspect his own load.

"The cemetery Lowes mentioned, right above, is home to Al-Sharahh's mausoleum."

His men paused, their eyes widening.

"Yes. Safe to assume they have a couple of patrol vehicles upstairs, perhaps tinted. This will conceal our Hazmat for a few."

One of the others added, "Until we're cleared of exposure."

Riz began suiting up after taking a sip of a cold sparkling water infused with accents of lime.

He replied, "Precisely."

The well of light flickered.

"Dark," a voice struggled from the edge of the access above. A mutilated hand reached for the ladder, never quite reaching as blood dripped from the severed limb.

Riz motioned for the men to hug the walls, his weapon trained at the exit. They all remained quiet.

"Cold. He di—" the raspy cry managed to articulate. The hand pulled on the bars, precipitating the rest of the body to a deadly fall.

Thump. The body hit the ground in full force. The voice never returned.

"Light," Riz asked. He approached the corpse. "Run it while Rich guards the egress."

A cold light swept the body. It was an older man, disheveled hair matching the chaos of an overgrown beard. His skin was dark and leather-tanned.

Riz crouched and surveyed the extent of his injuries, pensive.

"Bullet wounds. A couple of severed limbs. He bled out. We need to move. Fast."

The climb proved tense, Riz's weapon expecting another casualty.

It was a desolate world they found. Shaded under chaotic rows of olive trees, the leader peeked beyond the close perimeter.

The cemetery was under a green siege; fractured tombstones were overpowered by a common ivy that had darkened the once shiny white marbles.

There were more corpses. Not the ones long buried and deconstructed into a symphony of bones, but fleshy masses crooked in fear, their hands reaching for their throat, pulling their hair or tugging on the neighboring bodies' shredded clothing. Riz found beauty in the scene, in this intricate mural that painted the pivotal moment when life attempted to deny an imminent death.

Past the cemetery grounds, far out, an exodus had indeed begun. Displaced populations looked like a trail of ants journeying alongside a lake.

"The transformation... It's partial here," Riz whispered to his men. He crouched and scanned his surroundings. The hole they crawled out of led to a terrace overshadowed by a massive mountain range whose green hills felt unfamiliar. Already, his officers had followed suit and spread around.

"There's no movement, we're clear," one of the men shared. Riz nodded to himself and stood. He engaged a small set of stairs to a service road, the rest of his unit stacked on him.

To the left, the road curved right, flanked by other terraces similar to theirs; some housed mausoleums, others monuments overran by moss and more invasive varieties.

The death squad pushed forward, like astronauts unearthing lunar terrain through the lenses of otherworldly breathing apparatus. More bodies lay on the side of the dirt path, dramatic in their suggestions. Riz began jogging, a handgun at his side, ready to strike unwanted contacts.

At the end of the mile line, a small hangar stood out as an eyesore amongst the transformed surroundings. Inside, two vehicles were stationed parallel to one another, their bloated hoods riddled with holes.

Riz ran a hand on one and popped it open. The others inspected the small structure the four-by-four trucks were stored in.

He checked the engine, relay box and battery. The holes never spread to the windshield or the dusty mechanical parts that made for the essential pieces.

"It's tinted. VLT around fifteen percent. Looks like cheap dyes."

Riz Qurban looked at his man and echoed the sentiment.

He answered, "Ok. This place has been spared somehow. We'll need to find out why, or how."

One of his men found a set of keys hung on a DIY hook nailed on the corrugated walls. At once, they entered the SUV their leader had studied and ignited the engine.

A chopped sound quickly turned into a fluid stream as they

prepared to make a run for the Pakistani border, fleeing the obscure green disease.

6

SHH. MOTHER NATURE CAME TO COLLECT

Malia galloped down a dark, rich-soiled trail atop a Qatgani horse, flanked by Agda, *Baba*, and a small team of hooded mercenaries who treaded on her heels. They were all like living anachronisms, actors pulled from various timelines and woven into this present moment in a strange patchwork.

They were all headed toward a bunker in the desert, a black monolith whose carved calligraphy reminded one of forbidden magic. Around the mysterious structure, Earth was still shifting, spider-like leaflets tearing through the cracks of a fractured clay. Water seeped through the color-switching grounds, shaping timid streams that ran to the neighboring mountain ranges.

But within a half-mile radius of the access point, inside an invisible dome, time had denied nature's requests. The monolith and its immediate vicinity were left unaltered, impervious to the aftermath of Malia's high-impact weapon.

An aperture etched on the side of the monolith offered a decline that plunged into the underground. Malia and her men dismounted their horses and sent them away, seeking the entrance with a purposeful stride.

Straight stairs led to a small broadcast studio adjoined by additional rooms.

The equipment was of modern manufacturing, its design and associated cable management sleek, lightyears away from the pre-industrial state Malia precipitated Afghanistan into. A couple of women *Baba*'s protégé shared features with were setting up for a live feed, discussing parameters as they paced between the set and a small production suite located a few feet away.

Malia made her presence known by clapping once; the loud echo flooded the small chamber.

"Are we ready, sisters?"

"Strength has no form. Ten minutes," one replied. The other added, "Everyone's capacity is in proportion to one's knowledge."

Malia remained silent. She turned to Agda and smacked her teeth; he started a security sweep of the premises, one room at a time. She then shifted toward *Baba* and asked, "I thought about your words. On individualism."

Baba nodded quietly.

She resumed, "I made peace with it."

"That makes you whole, child."

A few minutes elapsed. Malia daydreamed of a place where she no longer had to compromise. The bodies of one.

Agda returned and bowed to the warlord. The two broadcast technicians approached her with caution.

"A hungry man has no faith. We are ready."

Malia looked around, then sought *Baba*'s eyes. He acquiesced and placed a hand on her forehead. She closed her eyes and let her mind drift away, to a green wonderland where mankind had found true contentment, where genuine human interaction and sustainability took over and became the driving forces of this sickly Earth. A world she may or may not be accepted in.

Baba released his hold.

"Are you in accord?" he asked.

"Yes."

Malia stepped onto the broadcasting set and sat in front of a camera whose orange LED light flickered in the studio's growing darkness.

One of the technicians stood behind the camera and raised an arm. The dimmed lighting cast shadows that wrapped around Malia's features.

A spotlight snapped; it enriched her aura and chased the shadows away. She readied, her brown eyes like amber spells.

The technician counted to three and pointed at her.

"My name is Malia, head of *The Hourglass Network*. I claim responsibility over the recent attacks on Kabul, Afghanistan, a set of strategically timed detonations that triggered a reshaping of the landscape. I understand that a red notice was issued against my person and that most intelligence agencies are looking into the matter. We will skip the usual formalities—the hollow threats."

Her eyes were menacing, however. Still impenetrable.

She inspired fear, on the prowl for her defenseless audience.

It was *her* narrative.

"I grew up in a remote section of the Wakhan corridor, a stretch of land bordered by China, Pakistan and Tajikistan. I was seven when a U.S.-led coalition sanctioned an air strike on my village. Was it warranted? Possibly. Some of the weaker men in my community had forged shady alliances with known terrorist groups. But in retrospect, I can only partially forgive the U.S., an imperialist and expansionist machine that bears no regard for collateral damage.

Indeed, the strike bore no fruit, ladies and gentlemen, like a young tree that lacked maturity. And it was kept from the public eye, under the broad and versatile label that is 'classified'. Yet, that day, on a starry night full of blurs, I lost many innocent friends and relatives."

Malia established a dramatic pause.

"But I have good counsel, a father figure whose wisdom has been invaluable in my quests. My savior. After the incident, he found the monstrous ideas that grew within me and trapped them. Although you may question my decisions—given your limited understanding—I have neither radicalized nor succumbed to madness, giving in to an insatiable hatred toward the West. We had our share of responsibility in the Taliban fiasco. Some let greed infiltrate our beautiful culture."

A brief silence settled in the broadcast studio. Malia glanced at her technicians and returned to the camera.

"But that night, the West returned. With a far more destructive intervention. Under the guise of a forever war, they desecrated our holy lands. The Korengalis will tell you. Resourceful partners turned mutants."

Malia's accusatory looks further sharpened. She was readying for a targeted strike.

A character assassination.

"Radioactive waste was discarded in our rivers, polluting our streams, aquifers, and banks. The disease that was unwanted exposure spread throughout the valley. I learned to view the drone strike that almost took my life as a forgivable offense, as an expression of the inability of foreigners to navigate our complicated customs and culture. But this crime against my land was more than an act of war. It was *us* versus the lower nature of your men, their basest instincts. So, I began exploring my options. Around the world, environmentalists claim the key to our salvation as a species will be found in balancing progress and sustainability. But there is one thing many people overlook.

Often, individualism trumps collective agreement... and such balance will never be achieved."

A pause followed, filled with a droning noise.

"I now have a power of attorney over all mankind's accounts. I elevate above the noise, above the petty considerations. To save this world from itself. Once I am done, I will address the cognitive dissonance many of you suffer from."

The feed cut to black. Malia stood.

Across the globe, viewers' reactions shot in uncontrollable bursts.

Her address had amplified the noise, pitting billions of channels that housed competing frequencies against one another. Biased opinions, wild fears, false equivalence, uncharted territories where learned behaviors were challenged, at once... all created mayhem that shrieked in dissonant notes.

The technicians approached Malia and stood side by side, obedient and stoic.

One of them inquired, "What of the hourglass that had been turned?" She gently struck her forehead with her right fist and bowed.

Malia reciprocated the gesture and replied, "A new life will trickle down."

She raised her right hand. Agda appeared beside her, silent.

Then instructed, "Agda, *kill*."

Two muffled gun shots rang in the broadcast studio, fleeting flashes only seen once.

The two technicians collapsed, sinking into an eternal sleep.

7

ENTROPY

"Sell!"

"Sell?!"

The frenzy sent floor traders back to the *pit*. The New York Stock Exchange was operating beyond capacity, verbal and nonverbal signals launched in the air like lethal vows. Malia's looming shadow had branded mankind with a wood-burning stamp, triggered terrifying realizations: the late-stage capitalists, the lobbyists, the *old money* peeking through the blackout curtains of their tax havens, all lost control of the narrative. Many had their intermediaries sell bonds, CDs, stocks, and commodities, with the exception of precious metals and minerals, whose value skyrocketed in a world that was believed to soon favor bartering.

In the deranged minds of traders, clusters and bridges fueled by narcotics and stimulants, many questions lingered as they all braced for the emergence of an economic model they would no longer game.

What about supply chains? Are we safe here? Sell SELL. It's over.

Malia's terror cell's threat, if founded, could effect changes over global dynamics, billions of lives, entire business models... Although her address focused on environmental concerns, it appeared this particular sentiment never resonated with the deeply selfish sharks who held their treasures so tightly they had forgotten to cultivate a different form of wealth.

"One hundred fifty on Lockheed. BUY! Sell two hundred! Dupont!"

Desperate evasive maneuvers turned the industrial superpowers upside down, exposing the hidden monsters of men and women who will possess nothing once the goods crumble and currencies lose their fabricated value.

On the trading floor, paper slips burst in dense clouds, ringing the sonnet of a war with no upside.

A beautiful, dark twisted fantasy.

At Sutton Place, a posh enclave on the Upper East Side, fair-skinned patrons had gathered in a private garden bordering the East River. The Queensboro Bridge cast its massive frame over the river's bank, swaying as if possessed by a debilitating fever. The men and women in attendance were dressed modestly, strangers to monograms, excessive branding, or flashy accessories.

A middle-aged man with round-shaped glasses was studying the East River's subtle current with a furrowed brow. In his mind, contingency plans overlapped like bricks laid on a makeshift wall in haste.

"Mister Delia? Pardon me. Miss Kelly arrived," an old maid announced behind him, her voice striking in deep, grave undertones.

He waved her away and turned around, inviting his guests to the white-stoned townhouse perched over the manicured evergreens they had set foot on.

A bronze door adorned with fish scales opened as he led everyone in. They all filled the space, drawn to a gigantic lounge area with high ceilings connecting to brown and neutral-toned walls. Paintings from various eras and movements crowded the surfaces, paired with sculptures mounted on intricate displays. The heightened perspectives and tonal contrasts gave the space a dramatic feel, like an ominous introduction to a world-altering conversation.

The families sat down as the house staff began taking requests for refreshments and bouchées.

The one they called *Mister Delia* let the scene run its course, observing the various responses from his relatives, their behavioral patterns as they argued a hypothetical apocalypse.

As the decision maker for the most influential and powerful blood lineage in the world, Mr. Delia never felt the need to confront petty issues only lower-class citizens were afflicted with. His existence was frictionless; he was above the law, above the guiding principles of men in society, above the abject nature of poverty and sickness.

He thought of this Middle Eastern woman, the young one. Malia.

She may be the one to finally topple the Order. To put a dent in this shatterproof body.

Fortunately, the patriarch possessed things beyond currency; he was owed favors, protection, people. It was time to leverage the assets his ancestors had poured blood, sweat and tears into. Just not *theirs*.

"Harris, would you close the door for me? Is the area secure?"

A bodyguard closed and locked the backdoor, a heavy twenty-inch steel panel that sank into its thick white stone frame. He checked his earpiece and answered, "The perimeter is secure. We have our digital *dead zone*."

Mr. Delia smiled and clapped. His audience turned silent at once.

All eyes were on him, some inquisitive, some accusatory, others neutral or duplicitous. However, he knew that the fate of their empire rested in his hands, and that even the most treacherous snakes would comply.

"It's imperative we leave the proxies behind and reclaim our name. It is overdue," he declared. The gathering approved with a silent nod.

"*Fuggers*. Let us have a toast."

They raised their glasses and teacups to the occasion.

"To a new world of intersecting opportunities. To the acceptance of unforeseeable events. To tragedy and wonders. To the resilient nature of our heritage. To our exceptional minds."

They took a sip and settled. The Fuggers' leader continued.

"There. Time is of the essence. What do we have?"

A short, plump lady raised her hand.

"My contacts in the Middle East have run projections. We have eight days, maybe nine before it reaches us."

The leader began jotting down notes on a small legal pad. The scraping of the ball pen filled the ceremonious silence. He pointed at a young man with a stately figure.

"Yes, father. The State Department has issued a notice. There are contingencies in place, but bureaucracy is the bane of doers. They won't make it, since there is a thirteen-day turnaround. We need to remain independent for the time being and survive the cut. Too much... Conflict... Too many... Contradictions. Our quieter location in the Hamptons is more suitable. We have a coastline, a lower population density, farmable land... I suggest we make the preparations now."

The ball pen began gliding on the paper. Many seemed to approve of the son's recommendations.

M. Fugger inquired, "I concur. Madeleine, assets management."

A tall and slim blond-haired woman sat on a chesterfield

sofa with grace. Her shoulders were straight, her posture of grand manner. She was a ballerina. Or a runway model.

"We're ready. Liquid assets have been converted and our commodities and goods are to be transferred to a location of your choice. I have implemented a few safeguards to ensure the process unfolds with the utmost discretion. That includes our art collection, here on the East Coast. I can attempt to transfer the rest, but it may not be feasible under the current circumstances. And a bi-coastal transport would raise further suspicions."

M. Fugger studied her for a second. She remained neutral and held his gaze.

He replied, "Okay. Scratch any transfer from anywhere beyond a three-hundred-mile radius. Keep it airtight. Ship the rest to our Fairfield Pond Lane compound."

The Fuggers patriarch turned toward his bodyguard, still as the night, hugging a corner that afforded him a clear view of the front and back entrances.

The chief of security answered the silent inquiry, "Sir, I will arrange travel for all members. Unmarked transport and shadow flight plans. There will be a security detail assigned to each itinerary holder. A small two-man detail."

The Fuggers leader clapped once. "Right. Agile and scalable. This is a delicate operation. The preservation of our legacy. This needs to be executed methodically and precisely. Bright minds at the service of a noble cause. All accepting of their fate, no matter the costs. No stone shall be left unturned. Are we in agreement?"

"Yes," they all responded in unison.

The powerful figure demanded attention from his housekeepers and security teams.

He added, "Bring your families. You've been good to us. Consider this a token of our appreciation. As Fuggers."

8

ANALOG STAGE

"K ia?"

"Yes. Right."

The CIA headquarters buzzed like a hive under siege. A composite of people and papers gradually built up, shifting to the rhythm of ever-changing parameters. Modern civilizations were on the brink of collapse—despite a valiant denial—and intelligence agencies constituted the last guard against a threat that was hard to quantify yet needed to be understood.

Malia had become *public enemy number one*, and most resources at Langley were either allocated to finding the drug lord herself, or to the development of a countermeasure for the progression of the disease, the plague she unleashed upon this world.

Kia stood in a conference room with suits, some of military background, others civilians. Acoustic foam panels drew wavy patterns along the walls and ceiling. A massive oak table cast refracted lights on Kia's rich sepia undertones.

She found a glass board erected behind her and began jotting down diagrams.

"Here's what we know. Malia and The Hourglass Network.

An ecoterrorist cell and narcotrafficking organization operating along a three-hundred-mile stretch by the Kabul and Helmand rivers, in the northeastern part of the Maidan Wardak Province. Tribal affiliation is unknown. Three of the key leadership members were scheduled for an air strike when the first ordinance detonated in Kabul's U.S. embassy. That strike was sanctioned based on findings related to drug charges and human trafficking, as most of you already know."

Kia took a brief moment to draw three circles connected to the words *Air Strike* by arrows.

She resumed, "As we know now, the strike was prematurely aborted, and mayhem ensued following the first *flameless* blast. Metals, concrete, plastics, engineered woods... all inorganic compounds were converted to organic matter within a five-mile radius, per our estimates. Thirty minutes later, the radius began expanding. It seems the ordnance has properties similar to time-release coating on schedule II narcotics. It expands over time, at a measured pace. At this time, none of our teams expect this expansion to halt, based on a timelapse we built off SATEL imagery. Malia, the *Network*'s leader, as well as two unidentified individuals closely working with her had no digital footprint until the recent events. We are currently working with tribal leaders to establish a background of some sort, but it might be too late given the time-sensitive nature of this threat."

An older man in military apparatus asked, "How fast does this... disease progress, precisely?"

"Our estimates are approximate given the lack of ground coverage. Most of the region's technological assets are down. A massive blackout. But we have between sixteen and eighteen days, according to our last forecast."

The man inquired, "Before it arrives here?"

"Yes, sir. And before we lose most of our capabilities. Satellites are also targeted. Some local assets have witnessed trails in the sky, above Kabul and the nearby western regions."

A middle-aged woman with a classy tapered short hairstyle and a flawless dark-skinned complexion raised her hand and spoke. "This is obviously something that we need to act on as quickly as possible. What is your suggestion, Miss Lowes?"

Kia established eye contact with her interlocutor for a few seconds, contemplating her options. She finally responded, "President Hardwick. I have already implanted an asset in the region, and he's well-connected. Two hours ago, I received a communication from him. He is alive, along with four other paramilitary officers. They are currently heading toward the Pakistani border. I suggest we leverage him to gather more information and locate Malia. But technology won't serve us here, apart from a final assault on the HVT and POI. We need a bold approach, minimal disruption."

The POTUS interjected, "Speak."

Kia replied, "An *analog* team led by my asset, with considerable resources at his disposal, Madame President. Old tradecraft methods, non-digital means of communication, an almost nonexistent electronic signature. A cell immune to this disease."

President Hardwick studied the faces of her contemporaries. She asked the military man who had spoken earlier, "Is this viable, Richard?"

The man turned toward the president, drawing interest from his peers.

"Yes, Madame President. Miss Lowes is an incredible agent and leader who consistently delivers, one I have the utmost respect for. I reviewed the plans prior to this emergency meeting and it's actionable, and the most viable option we have considering the unique nature of this attack."

Kia's eyes ran on the glass board, studying the various

factors. She drew a tree line with various trunk sizes, some tall ones sticking out of the emergent layer.

"Madame President. Let me expand on the analog approach. Those are trees. This is the gross representation of a forest. And a representation of the impacted regions. Most of those trees are of equal size. They would be your digital means, the ones we adopted in mass."

Kia drew more trees, stopping at the edge of the board.

"An infinite forest. A digital grid that covers the world. But now, those trees are looking for something, a disruptor. Malia. However, she is mobile and those trees being of equal size... they have very little visibility on the situation."

She circled the giant trees. "And those are our ancient trees. The ones that were established before and remained. The ones that no longer bend to the rules of this forest. Our analog means. And our human assets."

President Hardwick ratified a document that was laid out in front of her, shifting between the illustration and the clauses. She handed the contract to a personal aide camouflaged in the darkest corners of the room and turned to Kia.

"Okay. Miss Lowes, not much of a comforting thought but this is the most delicate operation ever conducted by our nation. The execution is time-sensitive, the outcome definitive. You have my full support but expect roadblocks. Malia is the first individual in the history of mankind to launch such an assault, and none of our foreign partners have been able to profile her, as you know. This is not the doing of a mere reactionary force, or a guerilla unit. This is the biggest threat this country has ever faced, whether nascent or progressed."

Kia agreed with a silent nod and replied, "Madame President."

All attendees rose. The room cleared, and Kia's vision sharpened, as a stream of faces and bodies rushed through the exit. Her sense of duty had trumped creeping fears and unsolvable paradoxes; it was her who needed to act on this, to try to curb the progression of a world-eating affliction.

She cleaned her glass board and left the oppressive space, soon poured into a hallway bathed in light. An older gentleman in a pinstriped suit awaited near a connecting bridge; his light footing matched Kia's like a shadow.

They remained quiet, walking alongside each other to an empty bull pen with comically depressing cubicles. Once a droning noise settled, the man addressed Kia, his hands pressed on the edge of a desk divider. "How did it go?"

Kia replied, her eyes dancing on the maze of supplies and landlines, "As expected. I was given the green light. But the chances are slim. It's most likely that the world as we know it ends in a week or two. Did you make arrangements?"

"For Trey, Charles, and Miss Lovejoy, yes. They agreed to follow us."

"What about your wife? Your twins, your cousins?"

The gentleman laid a gentle hand on her shoulders and smiled. He stared into her soul and confirmed, "We are privileged, Kia. They will be there too. Now, go and try to salvage this world."

9

THE PLAGUES OF KABUL

It was demons shooting across the skies, crimson strokes on dark hues of blue.

The girl's own face felt foreign to her, like a mask of flesh that never properly fit. Her skin burned and froze, as she yearned for more highs and lows. Her brain connections fired strong as she studied bodies ensnared in wild roots, beneath a blanket of tall grass.

The air was heavy on her lungs, a sweet scent rewarding every struggling breath. The teen walked Kabul alongside her handlers, with whom she shared the same characteristic gray pupils. Something powerful ran through her bloodstream, track marks puncturing her arms like wild constellations.

She began moving corpses, pulling them like stubborn weeds. Her strength belonged to another world; her small frame carried three adult-sized bodies leaning on the heavy side, with no signs of struggle.

"Amina! There," an older man yelled, pointing at a macabre pile of flesh set in a dirt clearing overlooking mountain ranges. She brought her offerings and returned to the man.

"*Baba*, when can I have more?"

The man was studying the teenage girl whose loose curls cascaded over thin shoulders, looking down on her like a smothering shadow. He glanced at the skies, his eyes shining in a bright grey, and replied, "This is not the time for feeding yet. Pick up the infidels and ponder their transgressions."

The teen bowed to the man and rejoined the group of survivors who had been blessed with the elixir of the gods. She continued digging into the wild forest, canvassing this brave new world.

Impurities. Seek impurities.

Before her stone-grey eyes, more dead flesh was uprooted, as scavengers began circling the skies, their wide wingspans fluttering with excitement.

Bones cracked under the weight of the piled-up mass, as the flesh tower found itself on the brink of collapse. The old man raised a hand, and all stopped, dropping their load.

He approached the pale cadavers and retrieved a box of matches from his cargo pocket. His slender hands picked a match and dragged it across the box's striking strip, producing an intense flame that expanded quickly.

Impurities.

A flick sent the flame to the pile of dead flesh and ignited the night with ferocious hunger.

The old man addressed his group. "Those who do not follow the prophet, those who clung to modern life like parasites... those are the soft monstrosities that melt like wax before your eyes. Ramza?"

The crowd answered in unison, "It *sees!*"

The songs of the wilderness scored Kabul's new videography, through a lens full of war fogs, colorful birds and shifting soils. A new society had risen from the ashes of a failing dream. The tales of ancient history, art and prose were buried alive and forgotten as mankind endured the treacherous currents of a figurative, tumultuous sea.

Amongst the dead bodies, a baby's cry competed with the Earth reclaiming of its throne. The fragile body was checkered with red marks, concentric patterns rising and falling like living organisms.

The baby's wailing intensified, thick curls laid on a round-shaped head whose gold complexion bound the dirt and the grass bordering its chubby flesh.

Glowing eyes studied the cry, the uncoordinated movements, seeking an opportunity to devour *it*.

"There's the child."

A young teenager in an immaculate silk robe of gold accents ran his scarred fingers through the newborn's battered flesh, matching the strange figures carved onto his crimson skin. The cries ceased, as the columns of time and space had seemed to freeze in this now quiet world.

"Shh. You and I are hope. Their future."

The mystery teen exuded wisdom in his speech patterns, in his containment. He lifted the newborn up and brought it closer to the delicate fabric of his knee-length top. His eyes had gravitated toward the moonlight, and spiraling fires roaring a mile away, ones that rose over strange shapes.

Others followed in his wake as he began a silent exodus, his footprint calm and precise. They were all wearing the mark of a shared transformation, circles within circles, ever expanding and retracting under a barely perceptible breathing pattern. They did not seem to exhibit the same behaviors as Malia's followers, the latter having subscribed to a cult-like mythos.

Though all young, their agile muscles climbing a newly formed ridge, they were *survivors*, wise journeymen and women who sought answers as to why they were equipped to withstand the harshness of a world that was reclaimed, repossessed by a planet many of their peers had violated.

But a higher power had planted seeds in their burgeoning minds; they knew of certain facts and hypotheses. Commandments and tenets that underpinned their duties.

Their leader secured the newborn, who found comfort in his matching scarred tissue, and engaged a narrow tunnel carved into a steep downslope.

"Peshawar. This is our calling. If you'd allow me. I can't guarantee an outcome, brothers and sisters. But we can try."

10

A THREE-VECTOR

KIA LOWES – LANGLEY, VA – BASEMENT 3

"It's progressing. Westbound. It seems it has spared the eastern front, toward Peshawar. This is where my asset is headed."

Kia swept the satellite photographs of a mountain range with a laser pointer. The black room and acoustic wall paneling competed with bright lights for the monopoly on heat production. Most present officials had taken their coats and blazers off, sleeves rolled up as they took notes in a frantic scraping of the mighty pen.

President Hardwick was immune to the general ruckus. Her sharp features cut into her peers' more rounded angles. She was reviewing a flowchart on a grainy paper her fingers carefully surveyed.

She asked, "Our POI, any sightings?"

"No, Madame President. We have reliable sources placing her in Afghanistan's western regions, in the eye of the storm. But there are inherent challenges to finding her, mostly technological in nature. Hence why we're unable to pinpoint her exact location or operate surveillance in the area."

President Hardwick cleared her throat, raising her hand to call for a brief silence when objections broke out. Her hands were following a web of channels leading to names, all color-coded in various shades of red.

She resumed, studying Kia and the satellite photographs. "There was no contingency for a blackout?"

Kia stood straight; her hands interlocked in the lower section of her boxy blazer.

"We do, but we've never faced something of that scale. This is a return to a pre-industrial state, beyond a targeted blackout. To protocols that no longer exist."

"Ok. What about your asset? And this... *Analog* op?"

Kia clicked on a small remote nested in her right hand. An urban concentration flooded the high contrast projector's screen, avenues and streets running through structures like blood vessels.

"They should be arriving in Peshawar within two hours. There's a safe house near the Dabgari Gardens, north of the city center. A remote area my asset controls. So far, hourly check-ins have been successful. I'm expecting another call in sixteen minutes."

Allegra Hardwick rose without a verbal cue. Others followed suit, yet still sought further closure through wide-eyed expressions and stunned looks.

She finally spoke, rearranging her materials. "We have an emergency crisis plan to set forth. I'll need a progress report in three hours. Anything inconclusive, and we'll consider a more militarized approach. On a grander scale."

MALIA – AFGHANISTAN – ZENDEH JAN

Hooded silhouettes braved a fiery desert storm whose sands collided with massive planes in a metallic pitter-patter.

The four C-130s were parked on the rectangular extension of a runway. Malia smiled at the chaos, considering the swaying of the wings that towered over her slim frame. Her skin was smothered in crimson dirt, as if bathed in blood.

Her trusted advisor and hitman both followed closely; their piercing looks shifted between aircraft.

She stopped in front of a cargo ramp, her lashes fluttering, small black butterflies trapped in a nexus of tan webs. The metal frame before her had remained immaculate, immune to the surrounding mayhem. She led her escort inside and found a quieter world beyond this *invisible* threshold; there was no deadly whistle here, no coarse grazing from untamed storms.

There, inside the plane, rested her army. Inert bodies that shared a central IV line and a constant, raspy *hum*. Medical beds were hooked onto the aircraft's frame. It was a symphony of wires dancing in concert alongside the walls, leading to puppets whose arms begged to be tampered with.

Drug fiends. Or maybe mental patients. Bound to detention mattresses, smiling as Malia entered the bay like the prophet of a newer testament. She raised her arms to call for attention and stopped at the center of the improvised ward.

"For you have been fed and heard. It is time you fulfill your fate, now, recognizing the privilege you were entrusted with. In exactly seven hours, you will swarm through the rings of fire. Are you aware?"

The men and women nodded in unison, seeking her frame through their battered corneas.

"Well. To further clarify, you will be the forerunners of a

new nation, a sovereign ideology founded on the ideals of a more just world. Ready yourself."

Malia lowered her arms and peered through the cockpit's aperture, taking notice of an iridescent sky that undulated in faded waves.

"Now."

The zombified cult members slowly rose, released from their restraints, pulling the needles puncturing their swollen veins, pressing on the bleeding wounds with emotionless faces of clay. The cargo's ramp shut, igniting the bay with fiery orange lights shooting from the ceiling.

The drug lord left her two associates behind, headed for the cockpit, toward the scintillant lights of a massive dashboard.

The pilot already in place looked over his right shoulder and handed Malia a headset. Her eyes found the chaotic skies once more as she readied to fulfill her co-pilot duties.

A smile cracked through the muddy crust imposed on her delicate features. The pilot considered her for a second, his furrowed brows raised at the unusual behavior.

Her smile crossed the captain's eyes. He nodded politely.

"*Agda!*"

Malia's voice thundered through the loud cockpit. Footsteps stomped the metal floor behind.

A shot rang, the muzzle flash lost to a shadow of dark drapes separating the cockpit from the bay. The captain collapsed and caved in his seat.

"Wrap him up and store the body. We'll use it for display."

The silent killer bowed to Malia and snatched the body from the curved seat, leaving his headset hanging on its edge.

"*Baba?*" Malia asked. A tall frame ambushed the aperture and took the pilot's place. *Baba* grabbed the headset and wiped off the blood splatters, muttering a prayer as he scanned the windows.

He caught a glance at his protégé, and returned to the cockpit's lights and switches, a partition of triggers, colors and beats.

His slender fingers reached for a switch above head, which he flicked.

Down in the cargo bay, speakers issued words with crackling statics. The plane's metallic frame had filtered the outside noise, now faint sounds of waves never crashing, or wind streams never fading.

Sit. We are set for takeoff.

Baba's measured voice issued a chilling order, as Agda put the finishing touches on his dead prey. The cult members seemed to show no concern for the cold murder, or the dead body, and complied like docile dogs, finding seats behind their medical beds.

"Malia? Instruments?" *Baba* inquired.

She looked at a few needles oscillating with the aircraft's light sway.

"Check."

"Radio and satellite comms?"

"Check."

"Global positioning? Make sure we're cleared from ACARS."

Malia smiled and reviewed the central console's display units. Their radar showed an overlay with a fleet of aircraft circling west of their position. The C-130 they commanded appeared as a blinking icon with the caption *Ghost: No Positioning.*

The sandstorm was raging outside, muffled through the ballistic glass yet persistent in its distant droning. The two marveled at the sight.

Malia placed her hand over *Baba*'s and asked, "Is the Eye still watching?"

A silence settled, inviting relaxing winds in.

A shredding noise broke the truce, followed by a loud thump. Quietness reclaimed its throne shortly after.

There was a contemplation. Eyes peering through the grainy veils, a war fog partially concealing a massive runway laid between mountain ranges.

"Yes, Malia. Ramza is a necessary evil. But in due time, we'll strike."

She nodded in approval and flipped a switch above head.

"Aircraft A, requesting status on fleet."

A few seconds elapsed before the internal radio system activated once more.

"Aircraft B, flight ready."

"Aircraft C, flight ready."

"Aircraft D, flight ready."

Baba raised both hands to the skies, palms facing up. He returned to Malia after a few seconds and motioned for her to continue.

"Set for taxiing. Prepare for takeoff speed. Make sure you're in *ghost mode—no positioning* on ACARS."

"Understood Aircraft A."

"Aircraft A, good copy."

"Aircraft A, this is C, good copy."

"D here. Good copy."

Baba pushed the central lever, thrusting the massive metal bird forward to the runway. Its wings were slightly bent under the heavy winds, making the transport harder to maneuver on its first left turn. Malia checked her side window and found the emergency lights of her other three C-130s, furiously blinking in the rising, blanketing sands.

Baba stabilized the plane and faced the runway's straightforward path, slowing down to a stop a quarter mile out.

He took over the radio. "Conditions are hazardous but ideal for concealment. Make sure you operate corrections at takeoff.

We need the cargo intact. See you at the rendezvous points. Aircraft A, over and out."

Baba turned the comms off and pushed the central gear forward once more. The airplane gained speed, rattling against the friction of invisible currents. The two pilots sank into their seats, collected and focused. The yokes were possessed by violent tremors, contained in *Baba* and Malia's firm grips. The former pulled his slowly while Malia pushed the central gear further up.

The C-130 took off, swallowed in the mist of a deadly shower. Malia's intense eyes sought the radar display unit; a devious smile rose behind the remnants of crimson clay, ones that clashed with the darkness of her loose curls.

TORKHAM INTERNATIONAL BORDER CROSSING – PAKISTAN

Tears and cries of desperation haunted the congested border crossing, semi-trucks and cars pressed against one another, exhaust pipes smoking by the closed gates leading to Pakistan.

Rifle shots rang in the air. The surrounding mountains were guarded by hooded horsemen whose shifty, fast-pacing movements foreshadowed an imminent crisis.

In a beat-up SUV that idled in the shadow of two massive freight trucks, five men were studying the crowds of refugees slamming the heavy gates, and the roaming guards nearby. Heat rose when bodies began collapsing, some trampled by panicked masses flooding in.

Riz Qurban listened to the many heated conversations in his vicinity.

His right hand rested on a handgun, as he watched lost souls being displaced by the emergence of a new biodome. The car rocked under the weight of a thousand rushing steps.

Riz's eyes danced between the refugees, the border's patrols, and other drivers.

"Too many civilians. But this could be our way in."

His men were quiet. He knew they were assessing the situation and looking for a way to insert into Pakistani territory.

He resumed. "We have four smokes. A breaching charge. Masses of civilians. Uproar. Confusion. There are feelings and perspectives to leverage."

The man behind him gently tapped his window. "Less security on the south wall. We could breach. Sloppy, but effective."

Riz turned to his men for a second, looking into the windows of their soul. His eyes found the driver and evaluated his commitment with a silent stare. The man behind the wheels nodded and placed his right hand on the ignition keys.

"Ok. Two smokes on each flank. North and south walls, twenty feet out. We can't use breaching charges to divert attention. Too risky. We'll breach directly through the south wall and head east until we find shelter and comms. Let's go. They're getting antsy."

The driver turned the ignition off and pulled a lever under the blemished leather of the car's steering wheel. The men dismounted, their weapons concealed under their floating tunics.

Desperate refugees swooped up the CIA operatives who split into two groups swarming toward the north and south ends of the gate.

A strangled blast and shattered glass caused a collective jump scare. Men, women, and children raced to the gates. Others pulled inert bodies to the side of the road, hoping to find them a resting place in filthy trenches drowning in plastics and waste.

Riz's vehicle was burned to ashes, consumed by the heat point of a million suns.

An effective distraction. He had veered right to the south end of the stone wall with two of his men, feigning panic while waiting for a sign to strike, from across the main road. The racket was nightmare-inducing, a deconstructed blend of screams, cries, overlapping side conversations and heat waves rising from melting grounds.

The acrid smell of their vehicle burning rendered the air even less breathable; a mist of darkness flooded the border crossing, punctuated by rifle rounds flying from every direction.

Suddenly, columns of a dense, white smoke shot upward across from Riz's position.

He and his men discreetly activated small ordnances tucked under their layered tunic shirts and threw them to their right, above a distraught flock of bystanders. They pushed forward toward the wall, exercising dominance over the shouting patrons.

Ahead, the Pakistani security forces threatened to fire at the crowds, rifles trained at crying mothers and children banging against the bars of a massive gate whose crescent-shaped pull handle rattled dangerously.

Smoke took shape on the right side, the faraway horsemen guarding the neighboring mountains fading in its rise. Riz and his operatives entered the smoke and crossed the threshold to the stone wall near the gates. He dismissed a few children who had found refuge in this quieter spot and placed a brown pasty compound onto the dry rock. A small metal plate equipped with a switch was embedded into a corner of the explosive ordinance.

Riz Qurban flipped the switch and retrieved a detonator from an inside pocket. They were concealed in the smoke, but a handful of outsiders saw salvation in the white screen, rushing into it, pressed by the security forces' abrasive tone of voice.

He and his men diverted the few brave civilians closing up on their position, shouting about a potential shoot-out.

Forty feet. Three-hundred bystanders. Locating us in low visibility... thirty seconds top.

Qurban's brain raced an internal clock as he guarded the breaching charge, anticipating more stumbling bodies.

Fifteen.

"*Sok ye?!* Aye!" A figure in uniform drew sharper in the dense smoke, his rifle trained at Riz. Arms wrapped around the soldier's neck. The young officer dropped his weapon and attempted to fight the lock. There was determination in his efforts, his eyes seeking help from the wall.

The soldier could not identify the aggressor behind him; deprived of oxygen, he finally collapsed.

Six.

Riz helped drag the body to a nearby trench, still engulfed in the thick fog.

One.

He returned to the breaching point and swept the sector with his men.

"Father? Is that you?" a rugged voice questioned in the chaos.

Riz answered, "Yes, son! Here." He clapped a few times before two more men joined their group.

Qurban approached the breaching charge and looked up. There was no pathway alongside the wall, no roaming guards.

"We're clear! On me," he shouted through the chaos. Riz ran back a few steps, guiding his men behind his slender frame, navigating the smokes. He turned away from the ramparts and flipped his detonator's metal switch.

A surgical explosion fractured the stone wall, consuming the bedrock in a concentric pattern. Riz and his unit rushed the newly formed hole, their guns surveying beyond the blast's dusty veil.

The CIA field officer swung right, leading his men to a

darker alley that intersected an unguarded portion of the fortifications.

Two miles down, the group slowed to a halt, hid their weapons, and engaged a busy street overtaken by an incessant foot traffic.

Here, colors were buzzing, sounds electric. It seemed Riz had landed in an otherworldly plane, one shielded from the brewing wars out West, and Earth's dramatic metamorphosis.

The men blended in the flow of hustlers, farmers, local construction workers, and the occasional shoppers. Black streaks on their silky tunics drew disapproving looks from the passing elders.

A block ahead, an intersection opened onto a road gorged with private cars and semi-trucks. Two-toned taxis appeared at regular intervals.

Qurban raised a hand and headed forward; two of his men crossed the street. The split groups reached the junction and called for cabs.

In a suffocating heat, they entered two separate vehicles.

"Peshawar, Shah Qabool colony Namak Mandi," directed Qurban.

The second vehicle followed his, and soon, both surrendered to an unforgiving traffic where dominance trumped courtesy.

11

THE EYE OF RAMZA

Power is exercised in broad daylight. But never reveal its true wielders. Note that you will maintain it from the shadows, however. It's a difficult practice, like maintaining soil fertility in lowland rice.

KABUL – AFGHANISTAN

"On the third moon, I, Ramza, had defied the odds. I had seen the duality of this world, and survived its sight. I was chosen to be the mediator, the immutable force that glues together the beaten flesh. And today, I'll usher a new dawn."

The massive crowds bowed down to a tall, slender man with a sophisticated combover. His ceremonial robe was adorned with rubies and sapphires. Layered pearl necklaces sat quietly on his long neck. Hundreds of his subjects had gathered before an underground entrance, a tomb whose inside glow flickered in the night. The speaker guarded its access.

He was peculiar. Significant, even. His followers presented the same symptoms as Malia's: faded corneas, the occasional tremors, rapid speech... but the charismatic shepherd, Ramza, did not suffer from the same afflictions. He was alert yet still, with green eyes bathed in a golden hue. His skin was brown and smooth, his jet-black hair shining with full-on thickness.

Ramza was a foreigner on his own land, a being that had not yet suffered the wrath of Malia's unparalleled attack.

He gently placed his hand on his forehead, palm facing the waves of followers erected before him. They turned away and vanished on a steep hill, committed to a silent and unspoken pilgrimage.

Ramza entered the mausoleum-like underground structure he had preached before.

His precious stones mirrored the surrounding torchlights and cast strobing flashes on his eyes.

Down a tortuous path, ancient carvings flanked his sides, expanding on walls that stretched into the further darkness. The murals depicted scenes of mythical creatures charging on horsemen whose spears cut into their flesh.

The beasts were otherworldly; they bore mixed features, from a lion's mane with snake-like slits for nostrils to a silverback's frame with tentacles peering beyond the war theater. Ramza's light footing barely registered on the crimson dirt as he ignored the visual wonders.

His hands and eyes were hard at work on the proper placement of his garments. Fingers straightened the collar, ensuring the chest stones were symmetrical; the pearls required a precise layout, the clasps and extenders aligned.

He patted his hair, stressing their bounce. A light probe of his facial features revealed a golden makeup foundation.

Ramza smirked, his eyes shining with a vicious spark.

The tunnel extended for a mile, before widening to a large crypt whose stone thrones sat on ground carvings that all converged to the center of the space.

There, Ramza halted his march; his intense eyes turned

toward a silhouette curled in pain, left to struggle at the convergence point of all seats.

Elderly figures occupied the thrones. One was left vacant.

The elders bowed to the speaker. Ramza reciprocated and raised his right hand. His slender fingers mimicked a rotation, sweeping the air with grace.

Boom.

Light breached from the ceiling, untraceable in its source, noiseless in its profile.

The curled-up figure was a child.

A boy bound to the ground by an invisible force, shackled to a terrifying fate. Ramza lowered his hand and established eye contact with his young prey. The latter was mumbling what appeared to be sentence fragments.

"Mo... Baba... you *Ahriman*. B... spirit," the child managed to articulate in a painful speech. Ramza waved him away, muting his complaints.

"Emissaries. Is the child ready?" he inquired in a suave tone.

One of the elders cleared his throat and replied, "Yes, *all seeing*."

Ramza approached the kid, a devious smile on display like the flagship of something more destructive than fear. He pressed his fingers against the child's face, trapping the tears that rained down his emaciated cheek bones, and pressed further.

"Thank you."

Pain manifested in the form of an eerie shriek, a high-pitched protest from the drooling mouth of a paralyzed lamb. Ramza sought the kid's fluttering eyes and pressed further to keep the boy awake. Black veins ran through the sacrificial lamb's flesh, in a facial cluster that shot in all directions.

"You will feed the *Eye*, breed new visions."

Ramza retrieved a knife from a holster tucked underneath his robe; the blade was of jade and the handle of refined steel.

The child's neck met the sharp weapon and began bleeding. Ramza's spider-like fingers kept the boy's head held high, a thick red liquid pouring onto the stone carvings of the ancient grounds they occupied. Gasping for air, the victim suffered from seizures as time ran its immutable course.

Ramza rode the high of his kill, his brain reaching an orgasmic state. He allowed himself to swim in a sea of clouds, to leap from planet to planet, more divine than ever.

All powerful.

Soon, a heavy silence settled, leaving room for new sensory inputs.

The cave was unusually hot; the sound of a heartbeat thundered through the sinister throne room. The emissaries placed their right hand on their forehead, in a similar fashion to Ramza's, while the latter released his hold on the lifeless child.

"It *sees!*" he shouted to the elders. Lights over this frightening set shut down as the murderer departed at a dramatic pace, rushing toward another tunnel access.

The passage steep downslope and dizzying, spiraling curves did not seem to affect Ramza's ceremonious stance; like the new environmental parameters introduced by Malia outside, it was simply a new opportunity, breeding grounds for the seeds of his glory.

The taking of a life or the tortuous architecture he journeyed through... those he had welcomed with sadistic pleasure.

The end of the pathway led to a massive cavity; a patch of dirt introduced a small body of water that bordered ancient caves and a space that housed Cold War-era electronics.

Grey marbles glowed in the darkness. Ramza raised his hand and motioned a rotation once more, lighting the cave bright, in the summoning of an unexplainable magic.

He addressed the small crowd that appeared before him, individuals who had been on standby in the darkness, lurking.

"Balance in all things. Unexplainable occurrences. Spirits meddling with technology. We are the beginning and the end. The middle stages. The good. The bad. We are *order*. Through me, it flows. It sees. It prophesizes. *Surrender*."

The crowd bowed and approached Ramza. A small mass of white robes traced his precious stones with discolored hands, unsteady fingers discovering the blood spatters that had stained the rich fabric of his garment.

The cult leader surveyed the still water found beyond his followers; it was clear, shallow, with an undefinable color palette. Carved steps provided access and exit on both ends of the underground pool.

Ramza advanced, dismissing his admirers. They quickly followed.

Soon, all submerged themselves and washed, gently scrubbing their fabrics and exposed skin. Whispered prayers flooded the basin, sung to the beat of short-fused ripples.

The one who sank the world.
Through Him I see.
Cleared of any wrongdoing for they twisted reality.
For I have withstood the storm, purified and whole.
Good thoughts. Good words. Good deeds.

Ramza turned his hand up and demanded quietness.

After departing from the water, the group stopped short of the electronics room, finding towels and medical scrub wear in huge iron tubs. They changed clothes, apart from the leader, and congregated around his tall, towering figure.

Ramza spoke, the crowd hanging on his every word.

"There's a threefold path. Control. Coverage. Conviction. Let us begin."

12

1980.100000

PESHAWAR – SHAH QABOOL COLONY – PAKISTAN

The night had reclaimed its rightful place in the clear skies. The city of Peshawar was a nocturnal animal, the moonlight reflecting on buffed car hoods, gemstones and shiny embroideries sold in chaotic streets.

Riz and his men had dismounted their cab, watching the cars disappear at the next intersection. Around them, makeshift shacks and wooden planks served as storefronts for aggressive locals who pitched their products and services with a diabolical relentlessness.

The Shah Qabool's slums were a biodome on its own, one whose heart beat to the rhythm of Father *Hope* and Mother *Fear*. The men negotiated the street ahead, a lively strip with hagglers who had a warped notion of personal space.

"*Lare na akhwa shai!*" shouted the *unit* as they countered various propositions.

The CIA operatives turned up a notch, syncing their behavioral patterns to the locals'. Their movements were almost theatrical, broad gestures with indicated emotions and manufactured laughter that complemented casual conversations about food, child bearers, and the economy.

Police presence was non-existent here, and the general population did not seem to care much for the life-altering changes the Western regions were undergoing, less than one hundred and eighty miles away.

Riz knew why. As a student of life, he understood very early on that abject poverty and a lack of economic mobility often acted as numbing agents for whomever stood in the eye of the storm. What's a deadly cataclysm to them but something they've all learned to cope with, on a daily basis, at an early age?

Life went on in this part of the globe, as some believed they were protected, while others patiently waited for Malia's engineered *disease* to strike. Survival was the only directive in this jungle, the only sound that harmonized with their sick bones and lean flesh. Riz veered slightly right at the next fork, a twofold path running alongside a trash-filled canal.

The moon shone on the sea of plastics and sewage spills, its craters' reflections distorted on the blues, whites and browns.

The men had traveled light; they hoped not to drop further bodies on their way to the objective.

Riz spotted a street sign across the canal, to his left.

430 Ganl – Dagbari.

He flashed a warm smile and shouted, "Ha! One block to beauty."

The men responded with thunderous laughter as they continued on the canal's dirt trail. Another sign appeared at the next intersection.

431 Ganl – Dagbari.

Riz stopped by the canal and pointed at a bridge that curved upward above the soiled waters, to his left; it led to another dirt path full of overgrown lots that housed fractured buildings, long-standing shells of the past.

"I have to make a quick call brothers! You see those lots? Ghosts!" Riz Qurban shouted. His voice echoed through the narrow bridgeway and the vacant spaces across the waters.

The neighborhood was a bit quieter here, the slums' soundscape now more of a fading dream than a lethal dose of reality. Qurban retrieved a burner from his concealed belt and keyed 143. His men were watching the waterway and nearby streets, suddenly less inclined to animated debates.

"Regency, how can I help?"

"Hi, this is Mr. Lang. I was scheduled for a maintenance call tonight," replied Riz.

"Lang. 143?"

"Correct. Coming for a five-point inspection."

"Great. One second please."

A hold silenced the exchange for a few seconds.

"Mr. Lang? You are good to proceed."

Riz raised a hand and struck his chest once. He hung up and crossed the bridge, entering the adjoining 431 *Ganl – Dagbari* street.

Above the narrow avenue, a massive tarp connected the small residential buildings found on both sides, shading the old stone facades from any and all natural light sources. There was no activity in the area, no signs of occupation, but a mile-long row of buildings crashing to a dead end. Riz and his team advanced through and surveyed the worn structures with narrowing eyes.

1. 2. 3. 4. 5. 6. 7. 8.

Qurban shifted right to an old wooden door with a knocker shaped like a ring. He hit it eight times.

Shortly after, the door opened, its hinges silent.

A young man of either Pakistani or Afghan descent appeared in the doorway. He wore serious black rectangular frames, and an olive cashmere sweater layered with a white dress shirt neatly arranged underneath. His dark gray slacks clashed with weathered sneakers.

A scholar, Riz thought. There was a feebleness, a certain fragility to his physical self. He was evasive, accidentally elusive. His dark eyes tangoed with the men's; his shoulders slightly raised. He finally invited the group in, revealing a large hallway of Botticino marble complementing green and gold patterned wallpaper. The entryway closed behind them.

"Hi. The dining room, behind those double doors." The host pointed at a set of steel doors at the end of the corridor. He advanced, casting furtive glances over his tensed shoulders.

Riz followed, trailed by his men. He watched the safe house liaison open the access with ease, yet briefly surveying its frame; as they landed in the dining area—a fridge, stove, microwave and a table—the silence grew louder.

"Lang?" The host asked.

"143," replied Riz.

The host sighed and sat down. He invited the men at the table. They all joined him, quiet.

"Strange times, uh? Badeed Ajab, enchanté."

Riz raised his brows and placed a hand on his concealed holster; one of his men, closest to Ajab, tensed, ready to pounce on the peculiar host.

"You met all the challenge requirements but you're not a field officer. Speak. You have ten seconds," threatened Riz in a soft, fear-inducing tone.

Ajab raised both hands as his eyes widened. He swallowed and replied with a cracked voice, "I'm not a great conversationalist, Mr. Qurban, so forgive me."

He paused.

"I'm a contractor. Environmental sciences. I was sent to join your team. The field officer in charge left. Most of the force was sent back out West through a safe route. You can check... Wit... With your reputation, I wouldn't try... wouldn't try you."

Ajab pointed at a wired landline mounted onto the bare wall across from him.

He resumed, "Key 0913. Direct line to Deputy Lowes."

Riz addressed his men. "Watch him." He stood and grabbed the landline, first checking for heat points on its boxy shell. Satisfied, he keyed the numbers.

The phone rang twice and *clicked*.

"This is a secured line. ID?"

"Lang 143. QR."

"Qurban? This is Lowes. You can speak freely."

His men relaxed, some turning their focus on the fridge, retrieving protein meals and water. Riz motioned for them to eat before resuming the conversation.

"Ajab? Is he vetted? Where does he stand in this?"

"Yes, he is. He received basic field training, tier 1. He's a polymath, a multitalented environmental scientist. Environmental chemistry, forestry and agricultural sciences, geosciences, oceanography... you name it. He's part of a new system we've put in place. But before we talk shop, I need to assess your condition. So?"

Riz raised a hand to Ajab and stated, "You're cleared."

He returned to Kia Lowes, his back turned away from the men.

"We're alive. I've never... It's unprecedented. It's a destroyer of worlds. We've seen people suffocating, falling apart *consumed* by the environment. It's a fate you can't escape, unless you're trained or else... there's displacement too. Thousands of refugees were trapped. A major humanitarian crisis, with the expected fallouts."

"What about Pakistan?"

Riz sighed. "Their border won't hold. But here, in

Peshawar? Life goes on. Poverty tends to numb the sting of extinction-level events."

Lowes remained silent for a few seconds, then muted herself. Riz watched his men eat quietly.

Kia returned, her voice sharper and louder. "How are you, physically and mentally?"

"Nothing major ma'am. Contusions, exhaustion, slight dehydration. A cake walk."

She laughed. "Great. Now, logistics. Do you have a pen and paper?"

Qurban motioned for Ajab to bring him supplies. The latter nodded politely and rushed to a nearby drawer.

"Yes, ma'am. Ready to copy."

"Ok. You're no longer operating under the DO. Your new unit operational designation is *Analog*."

The pen scratched the paper, its ball elegantly rolling to birth cursive. Kia Lowes resumed after a brief pause.

"Ajab may be the key to an effective countermeasure. The data is scarce, and you are the closest source at the moment. He needs to be protected, with your life as a trade-in, if necessary. You'll find a manual at this location. It'll help you with setting analog means of communication. Most below ground level, as we found out that whatever Malia, the person of interest, has unleashed has no apparent effect on underground systems and biomes. Do you follow?"

"Yes, ma'am. You are the direct report."

"Precisely."

A brief silence settled. Riz welcomed extreme fatigue like an old friend, ignoring the telltale signs of exhaustion he suffered from.

"There's also a brief we were able to send to your location. Operational details. Kill list. Contingencies."

"Understood. Were there other attacks? Or is it just Kabul?"

Kia cleared her throat and replied, "As of now, no other reported attacks outside of that region. But the environmental changes you've witnessed firsthand propagated westbound. It's progressing Riz, but it's somehow guided, like a precision weapon. We have limited surveillance capability there, but the last estimates placed the radius at about five hundred miles west of Kabul."

Riz processed the information, jotting down notes, diagrams and fighting off a sharp pain behind his left eye.

He acknowledged her. "Ok."

"Your mission order is a two-step, sequential. I need you to clear your kill list first, by precedence, from first to last. Second, I need you to assist Ajab in collecting data to manufacture a countermeasure. This is more of a long-term endeavor. Right now, we need to poison the roach nest. Proliferation and all."

Before Riz could question the methodology, Kia Lowes interjected.

"We understand that you have limited technological capabilities. You'll be outfitted with more tac gear. Delivery should occur in twelve hours. It'll come with an intel packet for your kill list, in addition to what you already have there. You'll go airborne in about twenty hours, five klicks east of your location. Per the latest intel, Malia is also headed east toward Pakistan. This could be a pit stop or her final destination. Regardless, you need to intercept her. The intel was vetted. Through ACARS."

Riz took a few notes and massaged his forehead. He asked, "What's your position? Not DC's. Langley's."

"We're already witnessing migratory fluxes. Eastbound to Europe and westbound to Asia. Wealthy individuals and their contingencies for the most part. Our GMD is on high alert and we're partnering with the MI6, Mossad, GRU, SFF, DGSE, Kopassus and Vympel. Something of this magnitude, we need a global force."

"But we're leading on that kill list?"

"Precisely."

In Riz's fragmented mind, data flowed on white construction paper; compartments were drawn, boxing each information in a specific category.

Kill list. Root.

Ajab's security. Imperative

Discourse. Incidental.

Malia. Ties.

Malia. Kill list.

"Ok. We'll set shop here. Thank you, ma'am."

"Don't mention it. Hit hard."

The line disconnected. Silence settled around Riz, as he felt the many eyes of his men laid upon him. He wrote a few additional notes and returned.

Ajab was quiet, his hands laid on the table, shoulders straight, proper stance with a slight formal touch. *Fascinating,* Riz thought.

"Clean up nice and rest. We're up and running in seven hours. I will brief you then."

The quiet professionals nodded in agreement and finished their plate in silence. Ajab readied to join them in the living quarters when Riz raised his hand and motioned for him to sit down.

"Forgive me, Ajab. I'll just need a few minutes."

The field scientist politely smiled and obliged, readjusting his glass frames.

"How are you feeling?" Riz Qurban asked.

The question seemed out of place, asked in a gentle and considerate fashion by a certified killer who had toppled a couple of nations.

Qurban read through Ajab's slight tilt on his left side.

"You were expecting a barbaric boys club with a complete

disregard for all matters science? This isn't Hollywood Ajab. We don't exist through tired tropes. How are you feeling?"

Ajab maintained his polite smile. He replied, "Quite well considering, Mr. Qurban. I'm honored."

Riz smiled. "Likewise. So, what do you make of all this? Our person of interest M.O? I just need to get a better understanding of the threat we're facing."

"Malia... the *Hourglass Network*. I can't quite *profile* her yet. Her accent, her inflections—there's a distinct Afghan resonance. I grew up in Jalalabad, so I recognize it. But she's articulate, with a remarkably extensive vocabulary. Yet, the agency has uncovered no educational records. And her motives... they're peculiar. She's an enigma, to say the least.

Her organization is atypical compared to standard ecoterrorist cells. At its core, it's a drug operation, with no documented history of environmental activism. Her last statements during the initial recorded address were notably vague. Typically, such groups operate from a deeply impassioned stance—rightly or wrongly—using precise data and established references. I'm not convinced she's a genuine environmentalist. There's likely another agenda at play. Or perhaps, other actors."

Qurban listened carefully, stoic, and soundless. He almost blended with the dimmed lighting and the ever-present night.

He asked, "What about the ordnance?"

Ajab drummed his fingers on the table and paused. "That's the interesting part." He resumed the drumming, though much quieter. "This ordnance... I reviewed firsthand accounts and studied satellite views predating the *Great Disruption* and it is... troubling. I must first identify the discrete chemical or microbiological entity at play here. And I still lack a live specimen. But it's rather a biochemical weapon. A new form of photosynthesis. Unseen before. Inorganic matter exposed to sunlight alters its own molecular structure to turn carbon-based, as in *organic*. If my theory is founded, any hidden underground structure is safe."

"Because no exposure to sunlight," added Riz.

"Indeed, Mr. Qurban. Yet, the scale and rate at which it's progressing. We can't just deploy localized countermeasures. And this *reverse photosynthesis*, for a lack of better terms, also affects atmospheric composition, hence our ability to breathe, among other things. Picture this—Earth, even considering its most inviting spots, quickly becomes a non-permissive environment."

Riz laughed. Ajab's brows rose. The former explained, "Earlier, you mentioned not being a great conversationalist."

Ajab sighed, readjusting his glasses. "Indeed, Mr. Qurban. It's the science that requires it. It demands communication to exist, data to thrive."

Riz studied the scholar, and his awkwardness, his mannerisms that defied conventions. Deep down, he was no different, and he appreciated the company.

"Thank you, Ajab, get some rest. We'll get you squared away at dawn."

The scholar left the room with a timid nod.

Another lamb.

There was a storm coming. Attached to a plague of biblical proportions.

I have to locate this self-appointed prophet, Riz thought.

Malia was *subject zero*, the universal foe. She carried the answers and keys to the unfathomable act of war she had claimed responsibility for.

"A brave new world," muttered Riz, into the void of an empty place.

Off a cleaned plate, he rose and sought the nearest hallway, his mind absolutely smothered in a sleep-inducing fog.

He found a room; it was a spartan configuration, like a nun's in a secluded covenant. His battered bones welcomed the firm mattress, and the darkness of a dreamless sleep fell on his world.

Malia. Ties.

Malia. Kill list.

It sees.

A shrill, high-pitched warbling snatched Riz from the seductive embrace of a voracious sleep. He tightened his grip on his handgun and rushed toward the door, the barrel aimed at the ballistic pane.

Two knocks preceded a shaky call. "Friendly!" Other footsteps filled the hallway.

Riz opened and briefly held Ajab at gunpoint before lowering his weapon.

"Intruders?" he asked, calmly yet loud enough to overcome the siren.

Ajab nodded *in affirmation* as the other operatives rallied behind him.

He added, "Yes, Mr. Qurban. I was alerted by my watch. Came as soon as possible. I'm armed."

Riz left his room and swept the hallway; to his right stood his men, ready and sharp. To his left, the dining area appeared empty, framed into an arched doorway.

"Ajab. Where did the breach occur?"

"Main entryway, Mr. Qurban. Five tangos. Some sort of breaching device seen on CCTV. Every other wall and roof are reinforced."

Riz nodded with approval. "Standard since 9/11. They must have demands if they're using the front door, unless they know of our protocols. On me. Ajab, cover the rear, do not cross lines of sight."

The men stacked on their leader, Badeed Ajab carefully walking to the back of the formation. He tapped the man in front of him, which dominoed back to Riz.

The latter engaged the hallway, his pistol steadily trained at different spots under the arched separation. His footwork was precise, side steps and a low profile that strengthened the very core of his center of gravity. The CIA officers soon rushed to the break room, Ajab following the quiet storm that flooded the space in a masterful dance.

Between them and the entryway, the marbled floor had borrowed crimson shades from the emergency lights that triggered above head.

Riz looked at his men and placed a finger on his lips. He turned to Ajab and pointed to his own right ear, mimicking a cut with his fingers. The scientist approved with a nod and clicked his watch.

The alarm faded to oblivion, leaving room for a small, irregular rattling that bounced off the entryway.

Riz refocused on the entrance, surveying its frame as they inched closer. The rattle shapeshifted into a pitter-patter of tiny metals shuffling on the door pane.

Not your usual breaching charge.

In his mind, opportunities and contingencies cascaded into a flow of *ifs*.

There's sensitive information we haven't reviewed yet. A schedule. No other local assets. The threat is manageable.

The leader made an executive decision.

"We will stay until the flight is ready and we've reviewed all intel. We may be compromised, but there's too much at stake. We hold this position. You are cleared for kill shots, left to right. Leave the last tango to me," whispered Riz. He donned a balaclava, urging others to follow suit. One of the men supplied Ajab with a cloth headgear and motioned for him to step back.

Riz raised his arm and swung it from left to right, borrowing from the patterns of a pendulum. The men okayed and spread in a wide line across the hallway, forming a fishnet awaiting its prey.

The pitter-patter ceased. A click echoed on the marble. The red lights above head drew shadows beneath the men's eyes.

The door opened. Faceless black shapes flooded the place. Shots rang, flashes dimmed by the dark reds. The intruders collapsed like a flimsy house of cards.

Riz shot the left assailant in the legs, bloody craters taking shape on his trousers. The attacker lost balance and attempted a killing shot that Riz had anticipated, him and his men quickly veering right. The *Analog* leader bridged the gap between him and his target and disarmed him.

A loud strike hit the target's temple as his eyes shut, a brief fluttering of the lids predating a loss of consciousness.

Riz Qurban shouted, "Clear? SITREP."

His second-in-command locked the door.

"Door is still structurally sound. I'm green."

"Clear. Green."

"Clear. Green."

"Clear. Green."

"Clear. I'm green," Ajab struggled, tucked in a corner.

Qurban had grabbed his unconscious casualty, listening to what potentially lay across the entryway.

"One man at the door. Rich. Everyone else, retrieve the weapons, search for personal effects, snap an ID, and pull the files. It's time we prep."

He dragged the body to an adjacent room and propped it against an old ceramic radiator. Metallic zip ties secured the intruder to the cast iron.

Riz lifted his target's mask. It was a man, of German or Scandinavian descent, with a clean-shaven face whose delicate features did not campaign for a life of struggles, or the venture of war zones. He snapped a picture of his face and sought personal belongings hinting at his whereabouts.

The man possessed nothing; he owned no kill list, no business card, no receipt, bore no branding.

"Rich, keep an eye on that room for me. We'll be back," Riz shouted from across the small space.

He stepped out of the room and cut through the hallway to a study, where the remainder of his team had set up shop, placing folders on a rectangular table made in a rich wood of red undertones.

Ajab approached Riz and asked, "No personal effects on these men. Are we to inform Miss Lowes?"

The office space boasted custom bookshelves carved into the walls. Riz thought of the books as slices of life, priceless memories that may soon fade into oblivion.

"Not yet Ajab. We need to tread lightly."

13

OUT WEST

HELMAND RIVER — SOUTHWEST AFGHANISTAN — TEN YEARS AGO

The version of Malia that existed in the springtime of her life walked the luxuriant banks of the Helmand River, running her fingers through red poppy fields that smelled of spicy almonds. Nothing about her behavior and mannerisms indicated she was a more juvenile iteration, however. The fingers danced on the flowers to gauge the stem's health and tensile strength. Her eyes were sharp, her facial features devoid of any unregulated tics.

Baba strolled by her side, forever wise and aged. His profound eyes considered the river's current with a great deal of intellectual curiosity.

They both stopped and turned toward the endless waves of opium gold, red petals that covered an edgeless valley.

"Agda is with the Sisters."

Baba's gentle tone made Malia soften her stance.

"Ok, *Baba*. Are we going to Ramza?"

"Yes. He is like a magician, only it's *real*. The thing is... It's bigger than this operation. Beyond the sheer veils of this mortal plane. We are reshaping this world, Malia. We've accepted the very mantle of leadership over this Earth. The bulk of mankind wouldn't understand. Our actions may appear immoral to some, but in actuality, it's a fine thread we stand on. *Man* is bound to sever it. Ramza, on the other end, can reinforce that fabric and wave away their scissor hands."

Malia added, "Like the *Kuchi* dresses you brought from your travels?"

"Yes, like the strong tribes of women who travel this hell on Earth. Like *you*."

They contemplated life, their eyes staring into the horizon of red flowers, the same beautiful floral compositions that brought death upon this world.

The lucrative root compound for a deadly narcotic.

"We refined this product, Malia."

Baba looked up at the fiery skies and the declining sun.

"It's going to alter our respiratory functions. One variant will be distributed to us, another to Ramza's followers. The latter iteration is more, say, addictive and a mind *controller*. A perfected form of scopolamine was used."

Malia asked, "No selective effects?"

Baba nodded *no*. "No. Consistent across all subjects. Safe for us, *His* soldiers."

He looked around the field to ensure no one was watching and pointed at the skies.

The two paused, turning to the Helmand River, a wild stream of clear waters crashing against wavy rocks layered with shades of beige.

Malia smiled and spoke. "Allah is great. May he guide us to a holier place, rewire the rotten souls into better... dispositions?"

Baba replied, "Aamin. Your language is more complex and precise. I've taken notice. Keep our faith alive, but do not reveal our cards. Ramza is watching. The Sisters are preying on us. They must not know we answer to *one* God."

14

WOLVES IN SHEEP'S CLOTHING

"This is the air strike we oversaw before the *failure*. Her operation is beyond anything we've seen prior. Not even Noorzai moves at that rate and distributes at that scale. Two hundred fifty kilograms of pure brown heroin per day. And that's not including her stockpiles along the south belt."

Riz designated three photographs; they showed aerial views of silos and massive rectangular loads being transported through a body of water that darkened amongst the otherwise lunar landscape.

"We have a kill list, and we have a countermeasure to develop. The former takes precedence. What do we have on the drug trafficking angle, Miller?"

A dark-skinned man, whose face was weathered by the sun and tight curls bathed in a sumptuous silver coat, cleared his throat. He quickly reviewed his notes and looked up.

"There's very little intel, which is strange considering the scope of her dealings. There have been interviews with locals, in the Helmand province, but most accounts refer to her as *The Eye That Sees*—yes, capitalized proper—or *The Wild Messiah*.

Some form of romanticized trauma, embraced collectively. A *Folie a Deux*. A shared madness. I'm somewhat of a poet–"

The men laughed.

"But her profile stands out, truly. Over a ten-year investigative window, not one soul came forth. This is unheard of. Even Pablo would be envious. There's more to it than just financial incentives and fear tactics. From what I gathered, they actually *believe* in her ideology, faithful to her cause. Which means we can't leverage potential insider threats. We don't have an organizational pattern, structure or a way in. She is like a volatile compound. Our best hope is that she either falters, or that we find an asset not directly tied to her core enterprise."

Riz interjected, "But we have the ACARS ping. Her plane."

Miller resumed, "We do. But I'm not sure. Someone of her caliber, this seems a bit too telegraphed. Not fitting her profile. Is that why Lowes is kept out the loop? Boss."

Riz nodded with approval. "Partly, yes. I want to check with a local source that may be able to confirm her flight path."

"Okay. One more thing, boss. There was additional intel in there. She is scheduled for a pit stop in Islamabad. Not sure how it's possible but the data seems accurate. There's a mention of Ramza, named like the compound we breached before the *failure*. 'Ramza will welcome her with great fortitude.' No further information."

Riz jotted down notes, scribbling bullet points on a legal pad.

He asked, "Anything else?"

Ajab raised his hand, sweeping a few reports that had been annotated.

"Yes, Mr. Qurban. As I noted before, there are contradictions found within her very own speech patterns. To the public eye, she is... *hm*... a revolutionary. An agent of change. She is making the decisions governmental bodies can't assume. Right.

And although she's holding herself accountable—to some extent —and appears a bit more nuanced, layered than your average warlord, there are other points of contention. Diverting from this specific profile."

The men listened, absorbed in notes they were inking on white paper.

"First, *dissociation*. The Hourglass Network—also, capitalized proper—is built off a drug trafficking organization, one falling under 'Continuing Criminal Enterprise Statute'. But there's no public record or admission of this name prior to her first speech. It's an eco-terrorist cell to her viewership, no less, no more. There's no mention of narcotics, or shady affiliations. She wants the focus to be on her recent actions, not her past history."

The men agreed with a collective *hm* and motioned for him to resume.

"There's also some form of showmanship, Mr. Qurban. The footage of her speech is clear, her wording and pacing precise. With proper lighting and framing. It was even color graded. And last, her foreshadowing threat. She is going to address our 'cognitive dissonance', as she put it."

Riz asked, "What does that tell you? How is it relevant to our objectives?"

Ajab laid two hands on the table, palms resting flat on the rich wood.

"I'm sorry. I tend to want to establish patterns first. What that means is that she is not simply reacting. There is a strong desire to produce something long-lasting. A legacy."

He paused for a second, allowing the men to forge nascent opinions and theories.

"Those changes she pioneered. The Earth being *transformed*. This is her legacy. She would want for it to go through. For this enterprise to *survive* her passing. Once you neutralize her, we'll have to face another threat. The elusive monster that swallows vital infrastructures, that disrupts entire ecosystems and orchestrates the murdering of world citizens, *en masse.* You need to make sure you keep that in mind, Mr. Qurban. This is a marathon, not a sprint."

A silence fell on them, a blanketing agent that brought forth new sounds, in this quiet study that carried slices of life.

Riz considered Ajab with professional interest, peering into his soul, attempting to break the barrier set by his thick eyeframes.

He resumed, rising from his chair. "Duly noted, Ajab. Call it PR, or optics. A wolf in sheep's clothing."

His legal pad bore a more extensive bulleted list.

"I will contact Lowes to confirm our flight plan and review a few logistical details. But otherwise, we keep the info contained for now. No communication with any external agent. I will handle it. Ajab, you're going to brief Rich while Miller takes care of the forensics from our unfortunate... encounter. Were the surveillance feeds transmitted to HQ?"

Ajab smiled. "No. It's a closed circuit."

Riz approved with a subtle nod. "Good. Miller, scrap everything. I want deniable plausibility. Like we never encountered those men. Everyone else, come with me."

The others rose and followed Riz. Ajab remained at the table, reviewing further intel and rearranging folders in a cascade of causes and effects.

In the hallway, Riz paused; he beckoned Rich, the man guarding the entrance, to enter the study. The latter was quickly replaced by another member of Riz's team, his gun trained at the door frame.

"Peace be unto you, Rich," stated Riz as his loyal watchdog passed by. The latter nodded in agreement.

The hallway traffic shifted to an adjacent room under Riz Qurban's drive.

Soon, they gathered around the prisoner, the one who was left to battle his intrusive thoughts and growing fears alone.

The CIA operatives stood behind Riz, their leader facing the prisoner in an upright posture, shoulders squared, assuming a contrapposto on his left foot. The shift in weight drew the prisoner's attention. Riz cut his ties and stepped back.

He shouted, "Shots! Friendly!" then drew his handgun and squeezed the trigger in an earth-shattering bang with the same frequency replicated in three subsequent shots. The hollow tips perforated the prisoner's upper thighs and lower calves, calling for the eerie song of his grinding teeth.

"I'm known for efficiency. I don't believe in democracy, much less in bureaucracy. Interchangeable terms, if you ask me. Do you value your life?"

The prisoner boiled with rage, fighting the blinding pains that shot upward through his flesh. His skin was red, blood rushing to the outer layers, answering a desperate call.

Profusely sweating, he had soon crossed a new threshold: loss of control.

One more shot burst from Riz's gun, tearing the detainee's lower abdomen.

"There was a study conducted in the eighties, pointing to a ninety-seven point three per cent survival rate amongst patients with penetrating gunshot wounds of the abdomen. Quite high, surprisingly. I studied the report. I know exactly where to hit. I may not be as precise next time, though. I may... Let my demons roam free."

Riz's tone was gentle, soft, and measured. It was the steady speech pattern of a scholar, someone who had been caught up in the many layers of their own intellect.

"Do you value your life?" repeated Riz.

The man failed to repress a tsunami of tears. He struggled a *yes* with a nod.

"Great. We have very little time before your chances of survival drop considerably. Thirteen minutes, give or take. It's not an exact science."

Riz paused. A few steps forward brought him closer to the man, his imposing shadow teasing the embodiment of fear, a quiet fear, one demonstrated rather than told, one given rather than sold.

Riz resumed, "Who sent you? And what was your objective?"

The injured sought comfort beyond the death dealer, clinging onto a focal point, somewhere on a bare wall across from them. He answered, drooling on the cold floors he embraced, "It *sees*! He has prescience and foresight. No amount of orchestrated pain can lessen its greatness. And once the world fa—"

"Are you affiliated with the sex traffickers who tried to rob our daughters of their lives? The Ramza compound? You followed us."

The man failed to respond, mesmerized by the very same focal point, the last bit of life he would partake in. He began smiling, mouth contorted in pain, a grotesque face performing under the influence of a violent distortion.

Soon, death came, loud and swift. And the dancing shadows that reigned over his crooked frame vanished in an ill-defined haze.

LIKE SANDS THROUGH THE HOURGLASS

UNDISCLOSED AIRSPACE.

"We crossed, *Baba*."

Malia had laid eyes on the skies, strokes of purple hues that announced dawn. Below, city lights vanished like commanded by a magical switch. The plane initiated its descent.

"Nine thousand."

The cargo bay behind the two was flooded with a dimmed red light drawing shadows on faceless silhouettes.

"Six thousand. Stabilizing. Manual-bombing?" asked Malia. *Baba* nodded in approval and replied through the comms system, in a measured tone that starkly contrasted with the all-around tension.

"Let's set it up."

They both left the cockpit and joined Agda in the bay, like monsters roaming the dark corners of the aircraft's frame. The medical beds were gone, neatly affixed to a wall of canvas and ratchet straps. Malia and *Baba* studied the zombified subjects standing alongside the metal structure, silent and compliant.

At the center of the space lay a device. A massive ordnance shaped like a layered cylinder, mounted on steel tracks stretching to the rear door. Its matte finish muted the surrounding lights, leaving its edges to blend with the darkness.

The bay opened, inviting strong winds that breathed life into Malia's followers. They turned to her, awaiting further instructions.

"The two closest to salvation, unlock its base," ordered Malia.

Two of her loyalists approached the ordnance. There was no reserve in their movement, no apprehension in their eyes. They rotated the heavy device with ease, pressing on the black matte finish.

Click.

The machine rose from its base and snapped on the tracks.

It was the work of a world-class engineer, a watchmaker from a forgotten land where craftsmanship had to be elevated to an art form. The two followers held the device in place, staring at Malia like soulless golems.

"Release," she finally instructed, her hands raised in an arch.

The executioners pushed the device toward the open skies, Malia following the object alongside its tracks. It quietly glided and separated from the rail, thrusted into the dark dawn.

Malia peeked down the open bay; the machine had stabilized in its free fall, deploying small fins that hissed like a giant snake.

A few minutes later, the sun began rising from its ashes, also peeking through the daybreak's curtains.

AT GROUND LEVEL.

The city had awakened to fumes, side chatter, and smoked

meats. It was a beautiful blend of modernism and history, bright, formal minds and street hustlers.

Eyelids were heavy, as bodies stretched to the rhythm of a new pursuit.

The skies quickly turned fiery against the backdrop of a faded blue, the morning dew keeping ground temperatures relatively low.

Above a forked path, a massive billboard read *"Only Allah as protection."*

Death ensued.

Thousand-year-old structures were swallowed by an invisible blackhole and regurgitated as vegetation and minerals. Bodies fell from the skies, dead weights incurring further damage in their wake. Blood shattered the cobblestones in millions of vessels.

A father and his daughter ran away from where the sun rose, attempting to outpace the devouring madness that had gained upon them.

"Baba!" the teen daughter shouted amidst the chaos. She reached for his hand as he readied to launch her to safety; they were soon engulfed in a sea of flames and dust, silenced by a soundless enemy no one understood.

Ahead of them, a few citizens were still breathing, fighting to evade Malia's grip. But a rumble of terror had caught up, a deafening sound that had drowned the pleadings and shouts. And shortly after, the atmosphere shape-shifted, seizing the skins and lungs, feeding on the few survivors who had found shelter.

Underground, historical bunkers were empty, haunted by the ghosts of past voyagers who had secretly congregated there to reshape the region's geopolitics. The attack was too sudden for the ruling class to flee, as they fell prey to their own machinations: the instrumentalization of religion while influencing the masses. They failed to foresee Malia's arrival, her piercing eyes looking down upon them, as a goddess who campaigned for universal retribution.

And there, in this lush Garden of Eden that regained its wholeness, the world turned quiet.

The sign that read *"Only Allah as protection."* was no longer.

16

SLEEPER CELLS. AGENT OF INFLUENCE

PESHAWAR — AFGHANISTAN — TWENTY MINUTES LATER

"I want all intel and tac gear loaded in five mikes! We have little to no coverage in this area! *ANYTHING* breaks out, and it's a solo act ladies!" shouted Riz Qurban, peeking into the narrow, shaded street beyond the entryway. His eyes raised to the tarps concealing them from satellite views as he imagined a world without digital trails, surveillance states, his occupational duties reduced to a sticks-and-stones warfare exercise. The prospect was both terrifying and seductive.

Riz departed the building, veering right, sweeping the surrounding windows with a long rifle. In the wake of his incursion, his men began loading a set of armored trucks that had seen better days, their bodies dented and headlights cloudy. A few impacts had created linear fractures on the windshields and the door frames did not sit flush with the vehicles' chassis.

Perfect, thought Riz.

Time slowly ran its course in the quiet street, the latter a window between volatile clouds and shadowy characters.

The CIA field officers mounted the vehicles. Their leader quickly assessed the cargo loads and jumped in the first transport, on the passenger side. They drove off toward the adjoining canal, their eyes glued to the neighboring arteries that were now bathed in a full, bright sun.

Riz retrieved a black satphone from the glove compartment and turned to his driver, whose eyes shifted between the mirrors and the road ahead.

"Encrypted voice traffic, low Earth orbit? I don't mind the transition between satellites if coverage is consistent."

The driver replied, "Yes. Verified the protocols twice. It's safe."

Riz powered on the device as the small convoy entered a backroad parallel to a congested highway access.

He keyed a number and brought the satphone to his ear, watching barren lands unfold to his right.

"Uncle?"

Riz repressed a smile. He answered, "Yes. I'm on my way."

A silent hold amplified the SUV's clanking sounds, its body and chassis swaying to offset its weak suspensions.

"You are cleared. ETA?"

"Fifteen mikes."

"Good. The ACARS shows our person of interest about a hundred klicks south. But we have a faster cruise speed. You'll board a Cessna Citation X. Are you familiar with the specs?"

The vehicle hit a small pothole; the landscape turned blurry.

Citation X. More discreet than a Gulfstream. Faster at high altitudes.

Riz acknowledged. "Yes, we are."

"What about skyjacking? From the control pitch?"

"Horizontal stabilizer? Forced entry?"

"Precisely," the phone operator told Riz.

Riz stole a brief glance at his crew and the second vehicle that trailed behind them, its contours at war with clouds of dust.

"Yes. We are familiar with the process. Quite ambitious though."

"Indeed. You'll intercept the POI's aircraft and gain control. They need her alive, but whatever other payload they have may be of equal importance."

"Understood. ETA ten mikes," added Riz.

The voice from the satphone hung up. Riz placed the device back in the glove compartment and swept the roads, once more. They were entering a more populated area, a mass of deteriorating buildings placed alongside a dirt road with exposed pipes that disfigured its trenches.

The sun glared down on Riz, reflected from one of the buildings above; more mirrored flares beamed the convoy, strobing at an erratic rate, following the trucks as they advanced along a treacherous route. Riz drew his handgun and shouted through his radio, "Possible spotters. Watch for any unusual clearings of the road!"

The driver was calm, his eyes floating in a gentle stream, swimming left and right. He sank into his seat, gaining speed and negotiating tortuous arteries.

Fuck. Riz sought the foreshadowing signs of an ambush, a sudden change in traffic patterns, bystanders, tails, observers perched on vantage points, unusual trash collection spots... but there were none. The bursts of light kept creeping closer, sequential, a forbidding wave that threatened to break out of its containment.

Ahead, a two-pronged fork suggested a wider road curving left, albeit an equally dangerous one; it was still carved into an urban hellscape, the slums faithfully watching the intruders as they rushed to their rendezvous point. Riz gripped his gun tighter, with blanched hands; his eyes considered various angles of attack, dancing with more fervor.

"Two minutes." His voice was steady and sharp, on the louder side. The strange lights still followed above, in an otherworldly exercise that defied physics.

"This must be automated. The synchronization is unreal. But *it* follows still. Stay alert! Look for a trigger!"

The lead vehicle swerved; it was a fine thread forced into a needle, the latter's bore a microcosm of careless pedestrians and deadly mazes.

Suddenly, the lights vanished.

A wave of radiance crashed into the building they had just passed. Behind them, the small arteries and irregular roads they traversed imploded, bursting into strings of matter under the effect of an earth-shattering detonation.

Both vehicles shook from the impact, the metal bodies nearly failing.

"Fuck!" Riz failed to repress a dry cough, clearing his throat as he peeked into the side mirror.

The second vehicle was still there, lost in a cloud of dust. Beyond its beaten frame, an entire urban concentration had been wiped out, reduced to ruins and thin trims.

"There!"

Next to Riz, the driver peered ahead, turning into a branching road that led to a compound.

An open gate flanked by massive concrete walls welcomed the travelers to a nexus of runways intersecting in a complicated patchwork.

Concealed by the blinding sun carried within the horizon line, a plane emerged before their eyes.

The satphone rang again. Riz replied, "Secured comms! We may be followed!"

The men in the backseat readjusted and placed a hand on their respective doors.

The voice in the satphone echoed through the commotion, "We have three elements for sec here. Bring Ajab and your cargo first."

Riz hung up and clicked his radio, "Ajab, you will rush to the transport! The drivers will take care of the load. I'll be floating in between both vehicles until we take off."

A mile down the road, the private plane's fuselage rose above Riz and his detail, providing shade and clarity. Three masked soldiers stood by the jet's side door, armed with mil-spec sniper rifles.

The cars screeched to a halt. Doors slammed wide. The driver rushed to the trunk while Riz and the others dashed to the second vehicle.

Ajab had already dismounted, safely, running to the plane with the same strange seriousness and formality. There was no conversation, no further shouts, but rather a silent procession of gear and human lives.

His coping mechanism, Riz thought.

In the span of a flash, the runway was cleared, the trucks disintegrating, swallowed by the same combustible used by the CIA officers at the border crossing.

Riz turned to the former slums, now a rising mushroom cloud with arching tentacles.

One of the riflemen he greeted shared his fascination. Their eyes met against a painful realization.

Inside the plane, the cabin had been reconfigured to fit both passengers and cargo, the seats pushed toward the cockpit and grouped in sets of four.

A woman in a windbreaker reached out to Riz with a serious handshake; her bulletproof vest fitted snuggly under the navy-blue jacket. She carried a small flashlight in her left hand, routinely clicking on its switch. Riz understood and remained still while the light spun on his pupils, triggering specks that expanded and retracted in his vision. A manual blood pressure cuff was applied to his right arm.

The aircraft's engines increased their fuel intake, producing a hissing sound on the higher end of the spectrum.

"We are moving, gents!"

The woman pressed her now gloved fingers against Riz's neck, poking at a few contusions on his sweaty flesh.

"Mr. Qurban. I'm Gerstler. SAS."

She paused, reaching for his spine and ribs, seeking gunshot wounds, lacerations or signs of internal bleeding.

"It's a mad world out there. You were tossed to the wolves and expected to thrive, with no direction, no buffer. You're dehydrated. Freshen up, have a drink, and get some supper with your lads. Fifty-five mikes until interception. We'll go over the manoeuvre shortly."

17

WHICH HAND?

The death squad had been analyzing diagrams that blossomed into complex dynamics before their expert eyes. Riz stepped back from the portable screens, studying his operators, all absorbed in their materials; they were invested scholars who doubled as deadly weapons, neutral, immutable, unwilling to submit to fear.

Aside from Ajab, Riz knew his men well, familiar with their thought process where compartmentalization and contingencies reigned over emotional triggers. They believed in a straightforward path, one in which competency trumped luck, outcomes denied probabilities.

One windfall with the lucky numbers.

"We're on the intercept vector. We have ten mikes before we cross their navigational path. You'll be breaching their C-130 from the rear ramp. At twenty-four thousand feet. Cruising speed is three-twenty miles per hour. This is as precise as we can get, given the parameters we've been handed," Gerstler explained.

Riz returned to his own tablet; two vectors crossed at a blinking dot that belonged to one of the paths. Data populated in the top right corner, ever-changing numbers and words that fluctuated as the vectors expanded upward.

He asked, "Still no readings on the payload?"

Gerstler shook her head. "No. They must use some form of thermal concealment—remarkably advanced given the plane's mass. You ought to walk this path blind until you've got a visual inside."

Riz smiled. "What about *our* payload? Our intel?" He pointed at a set of black trunks placed near the rear section of the fuselage.

"We'll safeguard it until you and Deputy Lowes settle on a rendezvous point," Gerstler replied. "As for the manoeuvre, bear in mind that using explosive charges on a pressurised cabin could result in fatal injuries. Detonate it opposite the impact point, along the fuselage."

"Right."

The clock was ticking, small beats of ghostly echoes layered with the grinding of hourglass sands.

The plane breached through high clouds, finding a quiet place.

"Ok."

Gerstler raised both arms and mimicked hooks with her fingers. Riz's men stood and lined up to receive their gear. Ajab walked to his superior, somber, something troubling yet unidentifiable hiding in the deepest pockets of his dignified posture.

"Mr. Qurban. I'm a scientist, not a stuntman."

Qurban led him opposite of the gear storage, closer to the cockpit. Against the backdrop of a thick linen curtain, he sought and tamed Ajab's evasive eyes.

"I hear your concerns, Ajab. But as a man of science, you'd agree that logical reasoning is essential to most stages of life. As opposed to emotional responses. Right? We are cornered, chased out while seeking a public enemy with unmatched resources and a unique methodology. While time flies by, which serves them. What's the only viable option here?"

Ajab swallowed and nodded in approval. "Pushing forward, Mr. Qurban. In a literal sense, mostly," he managed to reply.

"Precisely. You will be paired with Rich in the rear to mitigate the risks. You simply follow in our steps. No breaching, no direct action unless deemed necessary. As soon as we neutralize our POI, you'll be able to get to work and maybe salvage what's left of *our* country."

Riz issued the scientist a piercing glance before returning to his men. Ajab followed behind, stunned by the prospect of a proper skyjacking.

The plane dipped.

He whispered to Riz, "Mr. Qurban, have you ever experienced fear?"

Qurban glanced over his shoulder and replied, "Briefly, in my younger days. A distant memory. It's obsession I cling onto now."

The men were outfitted with combat gear, including a lightweight bulletproof vest, and a breathable and flexible fabric manufactured with a rip-resistant material. Base layers were worn underneath to provide cold protection. An oxygen circuit composed of a breathing apparatus and a portable tank completed the setup, along with handguns, short barrel rifles as well as a tactical backpack carrying multi-purpose tools.

Riz checked his men's gear then requested that his gear be reviewed, pointing at his back. After a few minutes of a thorough examination, a voice took over the silent process with authority.

"Intercept in two mikes," shouted Gerstler, exercising dominance over the hissing of oxygen tanks.

Riz nodded and addressed his men.

"I will lead the charge. Alpha designations. Rich in the rear, with Ajab. Make sure he survives, Rich."

He paused.

"Once we get in, call your kills, if any. Direct action is priority, followed by an EOD sweep and a review of the aircraft's controls. How copy?"

All gave a thumbs-up. Ajab suffered a small delay but finally acknowledged.

Riz approached Gerstler and whispered, "How are you going to approach undetected?"

She smiled. "It's *nigh* on impossible, especially given their supposed capability. But our pilot's ex-Navy—they do enjoy a bit of rough handling. We're more manoeuvrable, though. It's a tight window, but you're well qualified."

"Hm," Riz muttered. He repressed a cough and headed to the exit door, followed by his men, docile and quiet.

Gerstler stood next to the door, raised her arms once more and rotated her wrists.

A voice came through the plane's speakers.

We are over the rear ramp now. No visual on the cockpit from this angle, and still no readings. Be cautious folks. I'm stabilizing. You have... five mikes.

Gerstler pulled the exit door, which slid toward her.

The winds were strong and abrasive, hurling a downdraft that felt like a vacuum. Riz held onto a curved handle to his left and leaned on the upper edge of the door frame.

From there, he could see the C-130's tail below, and his objective: a softer spot on the left side of the rear aperture. He turned to Gerstler and raised his thumb. She reciprocated.

The squad's eyes were concealed by tinted lenses, their expression of selves buried like deep, dark secrets. Riz's voice crackled through the internal comms.

"Check?"

"A2. Green."

"A3. Green status."

"A4. Green."

"A5. Green status."

"A6. Green."

Riz evaluated the distance between his egress and the plane below, estimating the safest approach.

A man can only measure to a scale he balances.

His thoughts leaked to an aquifer of religious considerations before he returned to the radio.

"Prepare to jump. Safe angles. A5, account for A6's weight distribution. I will breach in and head for the commands."

"A5, acknowledged."

Riz leaped forward.

His plunge into the skies' giant chasm led him below, where a massive grey frame offered a wider landing area he negotiated with finesse, his legs propelled onward with controlled momentum. He moved forward, battling an ongoing wind stream.

Behind, his men landed flawlessly; Ajab was holding onto Rich in the rear, adopting a lower profile to find balance in what he probably considered *madness*.

Their boots' non-slip soles provided additional grip, but the CIA officers had found the weathered metal of the aircraft's frame bonding enough to offset the dangerous wind currents. Riz turned around and passed his men. He looked above and saw Gerstler's plane drifting away, taking a stationary position on a higher point.

The rear area was quite large, far from its standard specifications. On the left side, the hull showed a small trap, slightly discolored.

"Found the spot! Prepare to breach! Find shielding and

advance on my mark. I have priority over the comms. Exercise *reason!*"

Rifles cocked, muted amidst the loudness of the high skies. Riz approached the trap and retrieved a charge from his vest. He slammed it onto the metal frame and inserted a wire into the soft, pasty compound; Riz motioned for the men behind to retreat. He took a few steps back himself, crouching, and held a detonator switch up high; it was connected to the wire through a small cylinder.

His finger pressed the switch, visible to all.

In this fugitive moment, the men's thoughts ran wild. It was microseconds of a continuous stream in which Malia, the person of interest, was the main flooding agent.

Who was she? How did she subject the world into kneeling? Will the answers die with her corpse lying on a cold metal floor?

"Banger!"

Riz threw a grenade into the blown opening. A blinding flash followed by a high-pitch ring foreshadowed his entry. He rushed inside the plane, his rifle sweeping the bay left and right.

An agile footwork delivered him forward, into the cockpit. The flight deck was active, instruments recording altitude, fuel capacity and a multitude of other variables. Autopilot displays showed a navigational path to acronym HND.

"Clear!" shouted Riz. He had returned to the cargo area.

There was no opposition force.

"How d—"

A condensation trail whizzed past the bay windows. The skies cracked, shaken by the detonation of an artillery shell, or a missile. The plane rattled, and soon, metal pieces pattered on its frame, like a light rain on the brink of fading. Riz rushed back to the cockpit and peeked through the windows; a giant ball of black smoke floated in the sky like an odd ghost lingering through the pillars of time and space.

Shit. This was Gerstler's plane. Riz called one of his soldiers and pointed at the flight deck. "Is it remotely controlled or left in autopilot? Where is it headed?!"

The soldier checked a set of wires left exposed under the yoke. He then directed his attention toward the navigation displays.

"It's been tampered with. There's an extra microprocessor underneath the drive box... It's remote. I've never seen that before, not for a vessel that large. The destination, boss... HND... Could be the airport code for Haneda airport in Tokyo but... there's no flight plan."

Riz gave a thumbs up, acknowledging the explanation, and returned to the bay once more.

"The plane is unmanned. I'm assuming Gerstler's plane was the target. She's most likely KIA. Radio cut out. Anything of significance here?!" he inquired.

Ajab took over the comms. "No, sir. There may be something embedded in t—"

A voice erupted through the speakers. It was foreign and elegant, seductive yet deadly. Juvenile and wise. At once.

"Mr. Qurban? This is Malia. We'll make this a rather short conversation since you decided to damage my toy. I'm not on this plane, as you can see."

There was a brief pause in her speech. Riz quietly motioned for the soldier posted in the cockpit to watch the flight deck.

"It's going to be a one-way conversation, Mr. Qurban. I did not outfit this plane with transmitters. By choice. Exchanges are quite inefficient in most cases. Too much deliberation, fewer decision makers."

She paused again. Riz began checking the storage compartments in the bay, looking for explosives and other hazards.

"You are marked for death. Between the emergence of a people that have embraced their roots, and the riddance of modern parasites, you have very little time left. Tools like you get discarded when the job is done, or when there's no job left. You may survive this flight, but will you survive this war? There's no telling. But someone like you, an executioner, has no place in this new hierarchy, this new power dynamic. We need visionaries, we need teachers, advocates for those who are willing to open their eyes and *see*. Whatever god or higher power you subscribe to... What options have *they* given you? This enterprise is beyond your comprehension, beyond the parameters of your feeble mind. You may be an expert at wielding violence with precision, but can you unify? Bring peace and breed common ground? Don't waste my time. Hide until you uncover a purpose worthy of this Earth. Or fade, forgotten, into oblivion."

An earth-shattering explosion took the men by surprise. The walls detached and burst outward.

Riz shouted, "Get dow—"

Sharp objects flew toward them, brought back by the shifting pressure and wind currents. Massive shrapnel ripped from the C-130's structure hit the group in full force.

The cockpit detached and entered free fall. The soldier who was left inside managed to slip through a small aperture and steer clear of the diving piece, gaining speed himself as he aimed to find a better position to deploy his chute.

The world was blurry, scents and sights blended into an overflowing *goo* of colors stretching beyond their boundaries. Riz stood somewhere between life and death, uncertain of the outcome, or the condition. A voice echoed far out, trapped within a veil.

See you... side, brother.

Life tore through his body, drawn out by the siren song of another shell, another lifetime, somewhere beneath or above the clouds. But within his broken body, within this cave that was flooded with darkness, a dancing flame had subsisted.

He felt his flesh burn, branded by a red-hot blade, and collapsed—his consciousness gone adrift.

18

BLACKBOARD JUNGLE

A JUNGLE – A FEVERISH DREAM – SOMEWHERE

eath will come. Why rush and oppress the soul?

It's a state of mind, the upshot to generations of deep conditioning.

It sees.

It's this disease, Mr. Qurban. It's insidious and asymptomatic.

Baba!

In the enshrouding murkiness of dark waters, Riz struggled against the suffocating embrace of an unseen monster. *It* was aiming for his chest, constricting his rib cage and beating on his screaming bones.

Down below, the outlines of a cityscape emerged from the depths of this edgeless ocean; buildings, plazas, and streets brought life to this underworld.

Shortly after the epiphany, it was no longer water Riz felt on his flaring skin.

It was the powerful draft of coarse winds.

Crash course.

The man and the mask.

His sight had faded to black, once more.

A developing, droning sound soon reshaped the wind currents; they were now puncturing Riz's skin in an asymmetrical symphony of perforations.

Suddenly, a commercial airliner broke through the surface above, set onto a crash course toward the cityscape down below. It was mayhem. A soundstage where physics had morphed into a foreign concept of blurred lines.

Flight MAL01. Prepare for impact.

Riz jolted awake, pulled by uneven strings.

He struggled to breathe; cradled in a soft bed, he felt a dehumanizing cold creep on his shell.

And then, heat rose within his bones' frame, reversing the course life had taken in a perilous exercise.

Reality set in, followed by an overbearing sensory input. Sweet scents, floral whiffs, the smell of wet wood... there were birds singing, irregular footfalls, crackles.

The colors followed. Greens, pinks, yellows, fuchsia... It was an intricate madness, palpable yet still so far removed.

Riz lay there, eyes lost in a strange, blue sky vault. Life returned within his patched soul, shaping his emotional state in waves.

Help! The sounds were mute, carving inward.

Kaappathunga! The carefully crafted phonetics echoed inside him.

Madad! A raspy cry dominated the vowels and consonants.

Fingers were now poking at his flesh, gently pressing on his carotid artery, his wrists, and the hard shell of his helmet. Riz realized he wore some form of protection and was viewing the world through fractured tinted lenses, colors appearing blurred or faded, shapes slightly distorted.

He died, he knew. Somewhere, up above, where his arms

would not reach, death had outsmarted and outpaced him. Who was he?

Q.

Miss Lowes?

Deputy Lowes in more formal settings.

My apologies.

Baba! Baba!

Contentment.

"Riz." His voice was feeble, still contained in the shell he was trapped in. His arms began twitching, fighting a weight he could not pinpoint.

The memories flashed before his flooded eyes; it was milestones, failures, celebrations, summer breezes and winter bites. It was the complexity of a being who had committed to the ultimate sacrifice yet fought to remain *human.*

Who is going to carry my legacy? Relieve me of the burden? Riz thought. Incomprehensible notions swam in a brain fog.

"Riz!" he shouted. The voice perforated the shell, as the strange fingers quit pressing.

"Mr. Qurban? Your vitals are gradually increasing. It's good. But... but... hm... do not sit yet. You need airflow."

Riz could not rotate his neck, which he felt was held in place by invisible pins.

"Who?" he shouted, his voice borrowing from strange inflexions.

"This is Ajab. You're in shock." A pause bred ground for a new soundscape. More footsteps crunched the nearby leaves.

Ajab resumed, "Your men, Mr. Qurban. I owe them my life. They're here."

His helmet gently slid off his sweaty pores. A warm breeze accompanied a blinding screen of light that flooded his sight. Riz's bleary vision progressively cleared to shapes hovering above him, shading his injuries from the sun.

Ajab's distinct, articulate speech returned. "It's a miracle you survived. A prime example of your remarkable conditioning. Blunt trauma, yet no internal bleeding."

"I pulled the chute before I blacked out," Riz remembered.

"Indeed, boss," Rich added. His men's shapes and features became more recognizable. Bears, freckles, wrinkles, scars... he counted four heads, including Ajab.

"Where is Bolo?" Riz asked. Ajab frowned. Rich helped him stand. Before his eyes, sunlight penetrated through a sparse canopy above, and a jungle floor below.

"KIA, boss. He bled out and crashed somewhere up the coastline. We didn't realize until it was too late."

Riz sought fear in the men's eyes, ready to assist in chasing the thwarting spirits away. But his men feared no death, no living being. This loss was simply an occupational hazard.

"I know we're dealing with the unknown and are pressed for time, but let's give Bolo a moment of silence. What were his five?"

"Running."

"Watches."

"Art."

"Jazz."

"Women."

The men fell silent.

A few seconds later, Riz cleared his throat and pressed on his joints. He had landed roughly, tearing parts of his jump suit, dried blood sealing some of the cuts on his flesh. But he was mobile, and the weathered bones he pressed on had withstood the storm.

"Where are we?" he suddenly asked, remembering the parameters of his mission.

"Indonesia. Natuna Island," Ajab replied.

"How do... You know? My GPS isn't loading."

Ajab stole a brief glance at their surroundings before answering. His glass frames were still impeccably set on his hard features.

"Notable landmarks in the regency. The black rocks you'll find under this sandy soil. Very peculiar carnivorous plants. I studied this biodome. I know its ins and outs."

Riz inquired, "Fortunate coincidence. Any urban concentration? Or outposts?"

Ajab nodded in affirmation. "Yes, uphill. Very few—"

Shots rang by the coastline downhill, concealed behind a thick emergent layer of coconut trees.

"Let's move!"

Riz struggled to find his footing, dizzy and beaten. He had witnessed death, however; in his fragmented mind, unspeakable thoughts had surged, painful reminders that he was obligated to support the pillars that held Heaven and Earth apart.

He began moving, gaining speed as he welcomed pain, his ill-advised companion.

A necessary one.

19

THE ONE YOU MUST NOT
SPEAK OF

"Unresponsive."

A medical light struck the translucent eye, highlighting black vessels that had progressed inward.

"We're able to synchronize the triggering of new responses with your vocal cues, along with the duration of the cycles, and the *gift*'s particular properties. You have full control yet able to isolate and activate very specific tasks, or parameters. More of a surgical approach," pursued *Baba*.

Up in the air, the C-130 evaded turbulent convection currents by sitting above cloud level. The sun set upon the heavenly skies, darkening the plane's grays.

Nostalgia hit *Baba* as he peeked through the windows. *Within*, voices competed for his attention, siren songs whose recollections whispered of alternate realities.

Ramza would have chosen another sacrificial lamb.

No drugs.

Malia would be whole.

Carefree, careless lives.

No green room.

No mass murder.

A voice elevated above the others.

One drone strike. One displacement. How regrettable. Ha!

"This won't kill them? Wear them out?" Malia asked, as *Baba* resumed his examination of a zombified cultist.

"No adverse effects. They may live a long and productive life."

He appeared pensive, showcasing a grave expression. Malia surveyed his sharp angles, his fatherly demeanor. She soon found his eyes and understood.

Agda sat in a corner, half human, half golem, immutable and inevitable. A gun sat on his lap, laid flat, barrel trained at the rows of followers who quietly stood on the sides of the cargo bay. His mind processed *his* reality as a nexus of vectors, clusters, and threat assessments. There were no feelings involved, no special considerations, no internalized monologues.

And when the master's voice rang, Agda sought the pathway that provided the least resistance to forward motion. It was his function.

"Agda. Review the Parisian files," ordered Malia. He walked to the cockpit and took the co-pilot's seat, grabbing a brown folder set on the flight deck.

Malia walked the ranks of her small army. They were calm like the rising night, smooth sculptures of clay that bore no identifiable expression.

She stopped at the center of the bay, slowly spinning.

"Listen." Malia's voice triggered the followers. They turned their attention to her, now sharp and alert. *Aware.*

"The false idols have fallen. They thought that this movement, this ideology would not survive my tragic demise. They tried to take this plane down in a targeted scheme, unaware that Ramza is on our side, and that *he* sees."

The followers repeated, "It *sees.*"

Malia resumed, "The Eye must be allowed to peek through

all doors, and you are tasked with supplying our godly watchers with this leverage. Make no mistakes. Spare no one. None that doesn't belong to this pack."

Herd.

She paused. The plane initiated a gentle descent.

"Europe. The colonizers. The dynasties that hoarded wealth through the exploitation of people and natural resources. Man-made history has never been a concept we supported, even within the boundaries of our own kingdom, but... *this* warrants a more radical intervention. We're landing in an hour. Prepare to show the industrialist puppets what the Eye is to deliver."

20

SHE WHO HAD MASTERED THE SUN

Whispers in the shadows. Hushed inputs from the underworld.

Death angels had parachuted from the high skies, faces concealed behind respirators. Riz came to a halt and faced the coastline downhill; the enemies had trailed behind the rumbles of gunshots he had heard earlier.

More?

The black suits lashing down from the clouds cut their canopies off, wavy drapes now gyrating with the winds, absently adrift.

They fell through the rainforest's thick blanket, disappearing in short-lived wavelets.

"Man of science, go! Let the locals know I will repay this debt in greater measure. Remember your battle drills. One overwatch for every other sector of fire," ordered Riz, his eyes glued to the coastline.

Ajab acknowledged in silence, his footprints loud in the muted jungle.

"It's a downslope. They'll most likely flank on the eastern

front. More permissive." Riz paused, fighting a leg cramp. Pain manifested as a serious smile, contained and devoid of joyful sentiments. "We'll meet them there. We need to be flexible, swift yet cover enough ground to survive a frontal assault. Staggered file on me."

The men snapped behind him, his weathered eyes and rifle trained at the terrace of greens spilling before them. Intricate root extensions woven into a magnificent mélange of foliage formed dark tunnels from where the killers would reach.

She identified our landing pattern's forecast.

Riz kneeled, smiling in pain. His lungs spoiled with dancing flames, a pulsing affliction lifting his flesh.

To outsiders, he was fully functional, his long rifle steady and fitting tightly in his shoulder pocket. The backdrop of singing birds found no disruptor as the mysterious enemies remained beyond the immediate perimeter. Tree lines and rock formations concealed the group well, providing them with a vantage point over a few apertures running to the ocean half a mile down.

Riz checked his in-ear communicator; it had been spared in the free fall, tucked inside his helmet.

"Rear two, do you copy?"

The birds sang to the sun.

"Rear two, do you copy? You should be above us," repeated Riz, looking over his shoulders.

"Lead, my apologies, good copy."

"SITREP? Do you recall OP names?"

A few seconds elapsed. Down below, the opposition remained unspeaking.

"I'm in place. It's a small gen, maybe sixty pax. We have two overwatches for you to fall back on. Forty-five degrees east and south. And yes, affirmative." Ajab's voice had shifted, less contained, more juvenile.

Riz checked on his men. They were blocks etched in clay, then turned to stone; he knew they shared a common interest in pain management and preserved their energy ahead of a potential confrontation. When the monsters breach the jungle, the CIA operators would bear the burden of survival, and—possibly—alter the course of history. Riz still failed to understand how to safeguard this Earth, but he was certain that Kia Lowes had poured massive resources into his operation out of faith in his ability to overcome, rather than professional courtesy. She had a practical mind, and his anti-social demeanor stateside only warranted for relationships centered on results.

This was a vote of confidence.

He returned to his radio. "Ok, Rear two. Remember your godmother? Practice your tables before she comes through. Once we're done here, we'll talk shop."

Ajab acknowledged on the other side of the line. "Good copy."

Movements in the tree lines below interrupted the cryptic exchange. The overall dynamic was fluid, almost snake-like; *they* approached, black frames merging with the woods.

War broke out.

"Contact!"

Bullets rained down on the enemies, cutting through their wires and harnesses.

The air filled with smoke, and an acrid scent of spent gunpowder. The CIA officers switched targets with precision, their thumbs guiding their rifles' bore. The deafening sounds of rapid gunshots coexisted with the thumping of collapsing bodies, in a fragile balance Riz held onto tightly.

1. 2. 1. 2.

1.2.3.4.

The triggers' walls clicked in pairs and sets, synchronized with the agents' use of cover.

Shell casings curved through the forest like a wild river. Full metal jackets stung like killer hornets. The dirt was lifted by frantic steps, as heat built upon the smoke of spent gunpowder. The CIA death squad journeyed a narrow tunnel vision as they pulled the trigger on the only lifeforms they wished gone.

Soon, the faceless enemies turned quiet, and the shots more sporadic. Reality shifted to a painful high-pitched ringing.

"Ceasefire!"

Riz's men stilled, the remnants of the last firings now a distant echo lost in the jungle below.

Dead people.

A semicircle of inert corpses arranged like an abstract performance. There was no specific pattern, but rather crooked frames and split lenses.

And to the rhythm of life, one of the bodies jolted awake. Followed by another one. And another one.

"Cover!"

Riz rushed to a nearby rock, leading his squad to a depression carved into the soil. Bullet impacts had begun chipping the stone, seeking the CIA officers beyond.

As the shots went off, Riz noticed a pattern. There was no forward movement, no controlled shot, no collective targeting; he was facing pure rage, an unhinged expression.

An outburst.

Riz shouted through the radio, against the backdrop of earth-shattering gunfire.

"Rear two! Did you see that?"

"The... the bodies. Yes. I'd suggest you fall back. We... we can assist!"

Bullets whizzed above head. A biting heat sought the officers, licking their open wounds.

Ajab understood, Riz thought. This was Malia's doing, a test run by a drug lord turned mad scientist.

"On me! Fall back! Rear two, coming from the south!"

His footprint pushed deeper into the softer soil. Behind, his men followed, ducking and shooting over their broad shoulders. The enemy's response was erratic, their weapons' chambers shrieking in pain off a canvas of metallic sounds.

The men rushed, in a race against wind drafts and tortuous terrain. Massive tree trunks were staggered uphill, providing natural screens on their ascent.

The bullets stopped flying. Footsteps followed in an uncomfortable crunch. Riz could see a man-made trail leading to a narrow block of makeshift houses up ahead. Men sporting hunting rifles were posted on the first roofs.

"Rear two. Entering the perimeter! We have baggage trailing behind. Tangos with full-face masks!"

A shot rang as they passed the local overwatch, the bullet leaving traces of a booming sound.

One of the locals collapsed, vanishing from Riz's sight.

The other returned fire. Riz entered the block and found a small pocket between two shacks. Adrenaline kept his vision sharp, eyes fluttering to wipe away sweat and unruly tears. His men followed suit and found covers in intricate cavities.

"We apply further pressure! They can't keep sustaining gunshot wounds. We need to drive them to a breaking point!"

"Copy," the team acknowledged.

Riz listened to the firing patterns. The sounds grew closer, but the surviving overwatch ahead was no longer returning shots. He faced the ongoing threat, expecting empty shells engaged on a relentless hunt for his men. On both sides of the dirt road he occupied, rifles readied for the masked enemies, the shadows who had once denied death its prize.

They appeared by the overwatch outpost further down the path. Half-servants, half-monsters, seeking rich blood.

In the blink of an eye, as atoms decomposed and reconstructed, the CIA killers squeezed the triggers. They pushed forward, their hollow tips perforating brain matter, stomach linings and lower arteries. It was a burst of fire, a sudden precipitation that washed off the impurities of this Earth.

But in the confines of Riz's mind, shattered into a million splinters of monochromatic color, one thought subsisted.

How long do I have?

He advanced toward the bodies with his men, sweeping the neighboring rooftops and windows. Curtains swayed under the inquiring looks of locals. His hands found the shattered helmet of a dead shape and removed it; there, he met the glassy eyes that *defined* the casualty of war.

"No pulse. They expired," Riz confirmed. He tapped his in-ear piece. "Rear two, we're clear. On our way. I'm bearing a gift."

He looked around, his eyes falling upon the bullet impacts that struck the community's living spaces, disfiguring corrugated metal and plywood sheets.

The soldiers that had sworn their allegiance to his cause were left unharmed, scanning their surroundings for any suspicious movement.

"Burn all bodies. I will bring this one to the scientist for autopsy. Make contact with the locals and return to me. To this structure up the hill." Riz pointed at a more sophisticated construction built on the steep side of a rolling hill. "Return the brave overwatch men to their families and show consideration," he ordered.

The men nodded in agreement and dispersed.

Riz grabbed the corpse he had just surveyed by the collar and began dragging the dead weight up the beaten trail, his eyes tainted by the fumes of a taxing war.

THIRTY MINUTES LATER – PRELIMINARY FINDINGS

"Why aren't you guarding this town?" asked the doctor, a serious man with a dark complexion and a healthy thatch of salt and pepper curls. He ran a light through Riz's eyes, studying his response.

"Those aggressors, they have a precise timetable. And many enemies. No amount of resources can offset that." He paused and repressed a grimace as the doctor pressed on his back. "We're small, highly mobile, with a concealed signature and footprint. We won't cause trouble. But we need to lay low."

The doctor inquired, "With our cooperation, I suppose?"

"Yes. We'll still operate surveillance while my partner conducts some research. Have you heard of Malia? *The Hourglass Network.*"

The elderly swept Riz's arms with his light, looking for injuries. "News has reached us here, yes. Reshaping the world, supposedly?"

Riz studied the physician. He was unmoved. "We are working on addressing this issue. Hence their assault. You don't seem concerned?"

The doctor laughed. "We have access to information here, but we live peacefully, away from the West and your self-destructive ways. Most of your peers see a shanty town, we see homesteads and sustainable means of living. They see poverty, we see happiness and contentment. It's all relative. I studied in London, *Magna Cum Laude*, yet I've always yearned to come back." He paused to clean up surface wounds lodged above Riz's armpit. "So, whether the world returns to its prior state or denies her wishes, we'll be happy with the outcome. We'll have ways to survive it anyway, as we never needed much to... thrive."

He raised a hand to indicate he was not finished. "But Mr... Qurban? I pledged to an oath, 'Do no harm,' and you approached me with respect. So, we will help. Your scientist can use our morgue downstairs. I understand he is not a medical expert so I will assist with the autopsy when we're done here."

Riz nodded in agreement. "Thank you, doctor." He rose from the medical bed when a strong grip invited him back down. He looked at the physician, his muscles tensed, hands balled in a fist.

"Relax, Mr. Qurban. You have nodules on your spinal column. Two small firm lumps, about one centimeter in diameter. Painful too, considering your physical response. How long have you known?"

Riz peeked beyond the physician; the room was empty, and footsteps heard next door suggested his men were still cleaning and prepping the body he brought.

The doctor's voice was low, and non-threatening.

"Seven months. I've been on medication to manage the disease. Tecentriq, Docetaxel and some others. But it's metastatic. They believed it was environmental. We couldn't pinpoint the root cause."

The doctor laid a gentle hand on his shoulder. "Eighty percent of cancers are caused by environmental factors, Mr. Qurban. What was your precise diagnosis?"

"Bronchial cancer. I've also taken a cocktail of supplements, a breathing treatment, practiced regular exercise, and a targeted diet. But the latest circumstances, it... didn't help with my condition."

"Have you made peace with it, Mr. Qurban?"

"I did."

A silence settled between the two. Riz had no intention of falling victim to his own fate. He had accepted that death may be occurring soon, outside of the battlefield. Parts of him wrestled with the idea that Malia's threat may be salvation, or more exactly *retribution* for the many others who died from cancerous cells dividing uncontrollably, and those who fell prey of the industrialist *massas*.

But there was also the extent to which she, Malia, drove that shift. There were other potential consequences besides a reversal to a preindustrial state. Political intrigues, civil wars, new infections and diseases...

Riz snapped back to reality and asked, "Do you have anything to further control the symptoms? I need to see this through. How long do I have?"

The doctor's grave expression peered into his soul. "Natural remedies may be more suitable. Fewer side-effects. But I can't give you a timeline, Mr. Qurban. I'd need to perform a bronchoscopy, cross-examine your medical records, and conduct some imaging scans. Given your line of work, I'm sure your records are sealed, or heavily restricted. The useful ones."

Riz tilted his head in agreement. "Thank you, doctor."

TWO HOURS LATER – THE AUTOPSY

Badeed Ajab and the local physician reviewed a stainless-steel cart that showed a precise tools layout. They were both wearing surgical scrub suits with medical-grade gloves and shield masks. Their eyes lingered on a corpse laid bare over another adjoining stainless-steel platform.

All around, a natural bedrock kept the environment cool and relatively dry. Cold medical lights shone from the ceiling, highlighting the dead subject's features and disposition.

Ajab looked at his counterpart and inquired with his eyes, "What is your name, doctor?"

"Fadhlan. We don't use surnames here."

"Badeed. Ajab. Nice to meet you. I was tasked with determining whether *their* functions were altered by an unknown substance, or some other agents maybe. We suspect they could hold the key to a herd immunity of some sort. If we terminate her first, that is." Ajab considered the cadaver before his muted eyes.

Fadhlan, the physician, approved in a quiet nod. He powered on the microphone carefully laid on the stainless-steel cart.

"It is two thirty-six am in Natuna, Indonesia. Lead local examiner, Fadhlan. I am here with M. Badeed Ajab, operating on behalf of the U.S. government. We are beginning the autopsy of an unidentified subject believed to be affiliated with the *Hourglass Network*, a global ecoterrorist cell. Male, mid-thirties, Caucasian. Please note that the subject is bearing a scar extending two inches downward from the bottom base of his left eye. No tattoos, piercings, or makeup. No apparent form of surgery nor further physical alterations. Proceeding to a brief external examination."

Fadhlan carefully counted the bullet wounds on the subject's body and searched for abnormal growths on its superficial layers.

"I have identified thirty-one gunshot wounds, including seven with exit paths, which will be referenced by area and diameter in my reports. No further abnormal protrusions."

Fadhlan retrieved a long scalpel, Ajab patiently waiting by his side, observing the process with interest.

"Beginning with internal examination. Proceeding to performing an incision from the collar bone to the lower abdomen."

Fadhlan pressed his blade onto the subject's flesh, cutting through it and driving the instrument down. He placed the bloody blade in a bowl and retrieved toothed forceps. The tweezer-like tool allowed the lead examiner to lift the heavy tissue running from the subject's upper to lower sections of the trunk. An uncomfortable suction sound preceded the uncovering of organs. Ajab surveyed the layout, seeking irregularities.

"All organs classified as vital have been perforated. Subject died from organ failure and excessive hemorrhaging. Internal."

"May I?" Ajab asked. Fadhlan paused and stepped aside.

"I am particularly interested in the respiratory functions, as well as energy conversion. Malia, our person of interest, has developed a weaponized form of photosynthesis. I need to know if this subject has been exposed to a counteracting agent that could be employed as a *shield* against the shift in atmospheric composition this very weaponized photosynthesis incurs."

Ajab's gloved hands dug into the corpse's upper chest and raised the lungs. Small cuts appeared on the upper lobes, splitting open under a slight pressure from his thumbs.

He resumed, "Found irregularities on the lungs' upper lobes. Like the gills of a fish. Nervures on the inner coating of those gills suggest it is functional, perhaps?"

Ajab's fingers ran from the right lung to the trachea. The latter was darker than usual, dipped into a blend of wine and mahogany.

"It appears oxygenation occurred at a higher or maybe irregular rate. Fadhlan?"

The Indonesian physician inspected the organs placement and condition; he nodded in a silent agreement.

"Indeed. Unusual respiratory tract. Notable. The subject's initial tolerance to otherwise fatal injuries could be correlated to his oxygenation capabilities. Further tests may prove conclusive in demonstrating unusual capabilities."

Fadhlan continued his review, removing the internal organs

for analysis and samples extraction. He then skillfully reconstructed the initial organs placement and closed the body.

Ajab studied the samples laid on a table running against one of the bedrock walls. His narrow eyes found Fadhlan's.

"Fadhlan, we may have unearthed the key to this war. The turning of the tides."

21

LA VILLE LUMIÈRE

Paris. Georges-Eugène Haussmann's dream child.

A monument to the grandeur of the "almighty" European empires. A delicate sonnet of formal rhyme schemes. A symbol of prestige fashioned through the instrumentalization of Christianity, deceptive policies, propaganda, and the transatlantic slave trade.

Resources stolen from the motherland, men and women shipped like cargo, used and abused to carry the stones that will shape the hallmarks of an illegitimate power.

Paris. La Ville Lumière.

The narrow streets that carried the many secrets. The craftsmen who catered to the bourgeoisie. The fine dining establishments of high ceilings and gold finishes. The Art. The high fashion, the heightened perspectives of deep-seated boulevards with tree lines that arched over buses and bike lanes.

The constant buzzing of people in the most walkable city in the world. The life that unraveled, evading the grip of a twisted thread. The magical characters that were the winding, tortuous pathways lit by thunderstorms.

The smells, the dangers. The markings, the seals. Dirt,

trash. Sterile environments, well-kept gardens that bloomed in a phantasmagoric layering.

On *Rue des Thermopyles*, a distinguished gentleman in a cream cashmere overcoat and brown tassel loafers casually strolled the beautiful, cobbled street harboring small houses with colorful doors and shutters. Wisteria and Ivy covered the stone façades, swaying under the light breeze of an unusually cold front.

His beard was neatly trimmed, the moisturizing shine sparkling under a combative sun. The clicking of his heels bounced against the asymmetrical patterns of ancient rocks, creating a distinctive echo of deep bass and high-pitched inflections.

The man showcased a pearly white smile that whispered *consistency* and mouthed *success* in understated elegance. He approached a massive double-pane door with wooden carvings, stepped aside near a gigantic potted plant and turned to the skies.

Forward observer, uh.

Suddenly, the doorknobs rattled. The ceramic pots ground against the stones. Vibrations traveled through space, lashing down on this quaint little pocket of a neighborhood.

Something massive was approaching, a monstrous engine prepared to shatter the above and fracture the below.

The gentleman retrieved a full-face breathing mask from behind the wild-haired potted plant, smiling at the discovery.

A miniature oxygen tank was mounted to the front air filters. He donned the apparatus, appreciating the swoosh sounds of an object, or mass, that was dropping from the sky vault.

All at once, an explosion sent black dust into the air. A coat of ashes swallowed the buildings and cobblestones, targeting any artificial and non-carbon-based matter. Structures liquefied, muting the desperate calls of unsuspecting residents. Death found every home, breaching from above, as a legion of angels enshrouded in black dust.

Mother Nature summoned her full powers, leading a monumental shift. Metals and rocks fought their last war, like a jostling, clamorous mob.

The voices of those entrapped grew faint.

Soon, the black dust had eaten all synthetic matter, settling on dirt soil and flowery plants alongside a soundscape dominated by rain sticks.

The man's mask hissed at the proposition, his breathing more rapid.

His eyes opened wide to the spectacle.

Further down the street, the half-consumed cobblestone uncovered a nexus of holes, wide mouths offering a descent to the underground. The gentleman walked the desolated street, marveling at the new cityscape forming before his eyes. Vegetation sprouted in a time-lapse fashion, and a fog appeared; it flooded the lush layers of greens that sometimes blended with other, surviving materials. A few cries for help reemerged.

Before him, scratching sounds could be heard from below. He stopped, his eyes shifting to a hole carved six feet ahead.

A hand dug into the soil, at the edge of the cavity. A dark thatch of hair followed.

People crawled out of the underground, docile servants lining up before the mysterious gentleman.

Of all shapes and sizes, they shared a common affliction: their eyes were discolored, their muscles abnormally stretched.

The pearly white smile acknowledged their presence with a nod.

He ordered, "You have your assignments, for you've heard the house sparrows' calls crowding out the other songbirds. Go. Spare no one."

22

OVERVIEW EFFECT

Stanton Park had been taken over by a chaotic pattern of white tents.

At the edge of the green space, a fast-pacing silhouette flew through tree lines that bloomed under the protective shade of historical rowhouses.

"This is a secured line."

Kia Lowes rushed toward the next intersection.

There was no traffic. The empty streets cried their hearts out in somber notes as a storm began clouding Washington D.C. and its never-before-disputed status within the world's political chess board.

A voice clicked through her cellphone.

"This is Qurban. The intel was faulty. We were lured into a trap... It was an unmanned C-130 we hijacked! NO POI, NO INTEL. I lost another man! How do you want us to produce results in those conditions?!"

Kia looked at the sky above, pensive. Clouds danced on the glassy surface that topped her sharp eyes.

Malia was unreadable, unforeseen and too feral. Would the

failures of the old world trump the potential shortcomings of a new one? Kia was looking for a political and philosophical angle, positioning herself in the seat of public opinion.

"Riz. Your concerns are valid. The ACARS data was tampered with, at the highest levels. Our POI may have a broader reach than we initially suspected. I'm dealing with FEMA planning underground evacuations here, thirty city blocks consumed to ashes in Paris. Iran and Israel launching nukes, general strikes, and rogue elements hard at work leveraging the chaos. Oh, and mass graves. Our European counterparts are launching a counteroffensive to stop her but given the extent to which she planned this..."

Her voice shook.

"So, this is it? Where do we stand in this? Because we may be on the verge of a breakthrough."

Kia stopped. She signaled for someone across the street to wait.

"No asset freeze. You have access to virtually untraceable funds, and contacts in your region have been notified. You still have support on the ground, but the treasury may collapse soon. A breakthrough?"

"Understood. Yes, we have live samples from one of her mercenaries. There's a cult-like following, something beyond a reactionary force. Ajab believes it's driven by narcotics use. A variant of the heroin she distributes."

Kia interjected, "Elaborate."

"She has molded those individuals, transformed them by administering a substance that subjected them to... some form of control? They also develop resistance to gunshot wounds and blunt trauma. Things that would otherwise kill an unaltered body. The demographics are broad. Young, old, male, female... all ethnicities but mainly Afghan and Pakistani from what we observed. There's also an ideological conditioning occurring, but

I don't have a source or method yet. I suspect it's our individual or deity. The one they name *Ramza*."

Kia carefully listened, drafting an email. "Noted. What's the actual breakthrough, not just the process? Did Ajab find something actionable?"

Riz's voice crackled, fractured by intermittent statics.

"Yes. It seems this narcotic has interesting properties. The corpse Ajab examined, with the assistance of a local asset I'm working with, presented gills on their lungs, like fish and amphibians. Their body had already adjusted to the new parameters of Malia's imposed world. We crashed a remote region in Indonesia. No terraforming has occurred here yet, so that means…"

"That they can operate in all conditions, old and anew. Ok. Have Ajab send me the autopsy report and update me on his findings every hour on the hour. This may be our salvation. *Analog* was never designed to fight massive field wars or even insurgencies. Your objective is to remain in proximity with the threat, if you can't reach it, and gain a better understanding of its nature. I know you understood, as a professional, but I wanted to remind you that there was still hope on your end. Our systems will soon fail, but you may thrive still. Stay there until further notice. And stay alive."

Cherry blossoms swayed in the wind, depositing large amounts of pink petals on the washed-out concrete.

The skies darkened. Kia crossed the street to a man in a brown wool suit, his features indistinguishable in the surrounding gloom.

She hung up.

FAIRFIELD POND LN — SAGAPONACK, NY

The sun shone bright on the quiet coastline. Pedicured feet sank into the immaculate white sands. Flawless skin demonstrated no signs of aging, cocooned in a world devoid of stressors.

The Fuggers had finally relocated, looking to witness and withstand an upcoming cataclysmic event. The patriarch, their leader, showcased a smile etched in pure white. His eyes, safely hidden behind designer frames, swept the crystal-clear ocean.

A woman stood by him, sipping on a champagne flute.

"No sense in the property being upgraded to safeguard against this bomb's specs. It'll be chaos on the surface," she added in a joyful noise.

Behind them, a gathering had brought a hundred people to this land. A massive modern home with sharp angles sprawled over five acres.

The man smiled and replied, "Precisely, Lauren. We ought to maintain a low... profile. There's been talks. Paris is under transformation. Data suggests the U.S. may be her final target... many factors. Her own life path of course, but also our contribution to the industrial revolutions. Her struggle is commendable... but we see here that our ancestors played their cards well. Power and wealth, that kind of access... is priceless. We'll usher a new age while others scrap for leftovers."

The leader invited Lauren to join the remainder of the party. Concentric layers of security kept the perimeter safe from intrusion. Expensive dry-aged steaks and wild-caught fish sat on a lavish buffet radiating colors through the addition of fresh produce and sophisticated sides from world class cuisines.

It was free-flow service at a massive open bar spilling out onto the beach.

Their East Coast front was shielded from terror, from the

feverish scrambling for resources by a working class that had no access to contingencies.

Here, time was sweet to the taste and soft to the touch.

The patriarch raised a glass. Others followed. The elders sat still; eerie smiles grew more dominant on their leather tanned skin.

"To us, to resilience, to family," he shouted. Glass clinked in effervescence.

He pointed at the skies and resumed, "When or if the vault darkens, we'll head inside and move underground. We have eyes and ears in all major city centers. If an attack occurs there, I will be informed, even if that wire comes through more... *Analog* means. Enjoy your stay here. This has been planned for a while, with unmatched attention to detail."

The crowd let out an understated laugh; smiles complimented the flawless facial structures and *quiet wealth* outfits. The surrounding heat activated the blossoming of nearby orange trees, infusing the air with a delicate citrus scent.

The patriarch returned to the white sands bordering the calm waves. The horizon was peaceful, the Earth obedient and compliant. He had the support of other cells around the world, groups of privileged individuals who had also effectively leveraged and exploited their docile workforce. Some had already gone to hiding, evading an invasive vegetation and an agonizing death.

They had begun building the blocks of a new life underground, in safe havens drawing from the surface's high oxygen content and pure aquifers.

The first reports from those new colonies suggested the patriarch's careful planning had borne nutritious fruits.

Soon, he will be the one leading his people to a secret sanctuary. His thoughts raced to a quote he lived by—a statement that shaped his methodology: Nostradamus' baleful glance at the world.

The Antichrist will be the infernal prince again for the third and last time... so many evils shall be committed by the means of Satan, the infernal Prince, that almost the entire world shall be found undone and desolate. Before these events happen, many rare birds will cry in the air, 'Now! Now!' and sometime later will vanish.

23

SHATTERED SEGMENTS

COMM. DU MONT-DORE — NEW CALEDONIA

A newborn latched onto his mother. Tears rolled down her emaciated cheeks, running over dark bags that suggested a destructive blend of sadness and exhaustion. She had climbed a rocky hill where life translated to scarcity. Dry dust levitated in spiraling columns, conducted by a rising wind that foreshadowed a tropical storm, one birthed by the coastline down below.

There, an urban concentration spilled over the beaches like a parasitic organism. The mother's tears intensified as she scanned the coast, her eyes following the incessant buzzing of vehicles and pedestrians. She was a skeleton, bony edges wrapped up in a coarse robe, hair thinning, eyes carved into her angular flesh.

The skies grew dim. A whooshing sound broke out from above cloud level, like the forewarning of a reckoning.

The mother shielded her newborn. The air grew warmer and heavier on her dark skin.

A black mass fell on the coastal city and detonated midair.

The sound was another swoosh, followed by the calming noise of erupting rain. There were no precipitation, however, but black clusters of a fine powder that defied established gravity by shooting downward.

The newborn stuck his head out, fighting the protective embrace of his genitor.

The entire cityscape further below was leveled to ashes, melting upon contact with the strange substance. Screams called upon the mother from the valley's depression. Mesmerized by the transformation, she froze, attentive to the process.

Entire structures disintegrated, vehicles and roads reduced to fine grain and dirt. She no longer saw the people traveling through this maze, seeking shapes and frames amidst the chaos.

Another blast thundered, traveling to the mountain ranges she stood in.

"Non! Dieu, protégez le!"

She lay on the ground, her newborn tucked into her robe, crying his tiny heart out. The blast reached them and shook her bones, grazing her fragile skin. Her child kept on crying, putting his best effort forth in his quest for answers.

Suddenly, the ground shifted. Roots sprouted, dancing on the coarse robe as they bypassed the mother's frame. She stood once more, looking around, marveling at the sight of a lush jungle housing heavenly oases. The ghosts from the valley had ceased calling, now replaced by new, more appeasing sounds.

A deceitful paradise.

Quickly, the mother's lungs constricted, unable to expel air. The baby began choking, fighting his mother's embrace, one that grew feebler by the second.

Within eyeblinks, they were both on the ground, still, immortalized in one last display of affection.

MYANMAR – SOUTHEAST ASIA

A young woman whose jet-black hair gracefully cascaded over an emerald tunic crossed the threshold to a garden nestled in a bustling city center. She was alert, privy to unspoken rules shared amongst elite circles. More deep green outfits appeared beyond a row of thick acacia trees, their leaves and branches overarching the veering passage she had engaged in.

"Is Ramza aware, sister?" an elder asked, joining hands with the young woman.

"No, sister, for he turned away from the three best things."

Their brief exchange crashed to an abrupt end when the young woman laid eyes on the remainder of the crowd. They were all gathered around a massive device.

The strange machine appeared to be similar to the cylindrical tube found on Malia's plane, on her journey to Western Europe. It shone its matte finish, deep blacks absorbing the scorching sun that beat on the city's garden. The young woman carved a way for herself into the crowd and raised a hand.

A gate creaked somewhere beyond their small perimeter. The other sisters replicated the gesture.

The young woman spoke, measured yet loud and steady enough to assert authority.

"We will follow the same threefold path, running alongside its vectors of conveyance, trusting of its ways. And for we seek to gain clarity on why destruction predates creation, we will walk this path on solid footing, with unwavering faith and reverence."

The mysterious sisterhood had gathered facing the sun, nonreactive to its blinding glare; some wore a cord on their waist, one that was knotted three times over.

The young woman resumed. "Let us thank Ahura Mazda, for all creation is necessary and destruction momentary."

She advanced toward the machine, pressing on a display unit hiding on its shaded side.

The device powered on and displayed a countdown.

15.

The sisters stepped back, joining hands in a half-circle.

10.

The air grew warmer, invisible needles painlessly poking outer skin layers.

5.

A swoosh sound foreshadowed an imminent detonation.

0.

The machine shot upward and exploded in coordinated layers, in an earth-shattering sonic boom that appeared harmless to the sisterhood.

Around the garden, the city center came to its knees, steel frames and electronic stores crushed into a potpourri of fluids and grains. People rushed to exit the smaller arteries, in an attempt to outpace the destructive current that poured down on them.

The paved grounds shattered, opened wide by the aggressive blooming of multicolor floral compositions. Through the cracks, bodies plunged to their death, buried alive in green sarcophagi.

The sisterhood stood calm, immune to the device's terrifying effects, benumbed by a privileged fate they appeared to share.

A few civilians had made their way through the garden's high forged gates. Footsteps registered on the dirt paths nearby.

"Help!"

The sisters remained still, ignoring the desperate calls that rang a few feet away.

"He—" The voices soon faded into oblivion, surrendered to an invisible vacuum.

Amidst the desolation, the young woman leading the convent looked up to the sun; it was bright and burning, its crisp edges running against the backdrop of an intensely blue sky.

"Sisters. The Night is coming."

SAGAPONACK — NY

Ripples hammered on the stagnant water. The glass slowly drifted on the solid bamboo countertop whose parquet patterns gave the illusion it moved as well.

The Fuggers' patriarch stared at the ocean front through the windows. The waves were foaming, the rip currents wilder, less obvious in their crossing patterns. He was smiling at the omens, at peace with his unwavering fate.

Right.

A slender frame appeared behind, perched on the herringbone floor like a bird of prey. The gentleman's face betrayed no weaknesses to exploit, no burning desires to fulfill, no bargaining chips to leverage. He was simply waiting to execute, unmoved by the most recent developments.

The patriarch spotted him over his shoulder. He turned.

"Gerstler. Can you feel it?"

The personal assistant's eyes diverted to the glass on the countertop, one inhabited by tremors whose contagious fear-inducing nature did not seem to affect the servant.

"Yes, indeed."

The patriarch looked up and smiled, mouthing prayers that were silent to outsiders.

A moment passed, as the vibrations grew louder and the sky above the ocean more tortured.

"I received some news, Gerstler. And this confirms it. It's coming. Let's move."

The personal assistant nodded in agreement and pivoted on

his spider-like legs, walking toward a sunken living room, beyond the towering frame of an arched passageway.

The patriarch had followed behind. They both came to a halt in the crowded space, where relatives enjoyed Cuban cigars and the elegant, homophonic textures of classical music.

Gerstler activated an intercom mounted to the closest wall.

He clapped once and stated, "The Hour has arrived, ladies and gentlemen. Our patriarch has informed me that the *Arden* is nearby. Kindly proceed to rendezvous point Alpha. An assistant will be along shortly to input your data prior to entry into the facility. As ever, we have been reminded that cooperation and courtesy are the moral fibre of this long-standing family. Please conduct yourselves accordingly. Thank you."

The patriarch observed the flow of family members quietly exiting through a massive sliding bay window. Beyond, a lush parterre guided the crowds to a massive garden housing a greenhouse, raised beds of various superfoods, and ornamental plant sculptures.

Gerstler had trotted to the front of the procession to assist with the evacuation. The patriarch was left alone at the rear, considering the dozens of quirks and features found in his bloodline with curiosity.

Some individuals displayed contentment; others frowned. While most remained courteous and disciplined, he could feel an implicit tension pulsing among the crowd.

The ushering of a new era is always painful. Many factors, many wild variables and small probabilities coming to terms. Soon, they'll find peace.

His thoughts roamed free as he followed behind. He had expressed the desire to be the last to enter the massive underground compound his grandparents had built; they had predicted some form of world-ending, a nebulous event written in dark prophecies they had uncovered, deep inside mysterious ruins.

However, the recent developments introduced a twist, or a spin: it was the end of *this* world. The reversal to a more primal setting.

Footsteps clicked on the concrete parterre, the rubber of the wheelchairs gravely whistling. The twelve-acre portion of land accommodated the chosen ones with ease, leaving room for the many faces to breathe and peacefully coexist during this historical moment.

The patriarch stepped forth, bypassing the line to join Gerstler and his assistant. He was handed a megaphone and turned to the crowds, extending for a mile in the thriving gardens.

"We will now take your information, for our registry. You will be given access to specific quarters and receive further instructions via your digital watches. Those needing technical assistance will find aides downstairs. You can also *activate* the life alert devices that were provided to you in the event of an emergency. I must say... I am looking forward to this new chapter. This is an opportunity for us to reflect upon our contributions to this world, and the decisions we chose to endorse over the past three centuries. Some of you may have concerns about the current state of affairs, in this lifetime, and this rapidly shifting world. Rest assured. Soon, you'll find the answers to all of your inquiries, to your most thorough examinations. I will enter last to ensure that everyone is accounted for. Thank you again for joining me."

A thunderous round of applause broke out, cheerful screams punctuating the standing ovation. The patriarch smiled, savoring *their* last moment in the outdoors before Malia's imminent intervention.

After a few minutes passed, he raised his hand.

The applause slowed to a halt.

The family members and handpicked bylaws began their new journey, disappearing into the stretched mouth of a doomsday bunker.

24

RIDER-WAITE: THE MAGICIAN

PARIS – FRANCE – LES CATACOMBES

A sign above Malia read *Arrête! C'est ici l'empire de la Mort*. Her nightly procession had infiltrated a world-famous ossuary where death reined free. *Baba* and Agda followed in her wake, shepherding a dozen bodies whose soulless eyes never shied away from their focal point: Malia herself.

The two men let their eyes wander on the arched tunnel, and the confusing layers of bones stacked within the walls—femurs and skulls forming hypnotizing patterns.

"No denying. This is rich history." Malia's playful tone turned fear-inducing when reverberating against the stones and cartilage. She carried a torchlight and a satchel, the latter tightly strapped to her side.

"Six million souls. All transferred from overflowing cemeteries above the surface. It's a privilege to witness such ingenuity, yet our duty to cleanse this unholy place. This unsanitary nightmare. But first, let's drink with the ghosts of a troubled past."

Their footsteps clicked within the echo chamber that was the ossuary. Sculptures of humanoid horrors studied the visitors, suggesting visions of a literal hell unleashing on the outsiders.

Malia's dancing light swept the cracked bones, the monstrous deformities, and other tomb ornaments. The underground was an ecosystem of its own, small insects thriving in low light, hidden in its corners and boreholes, the earthy smell of a humid cave whose air pockets hummed an indescribable melody. Names were carved on somber altars crowned in bones, accompanied with sinister phrases that borrowed from a prophetic exercise.

Et le monde s'écroule.

Nous les rejoignons bientôt.

La mort a trouvé le Marquis.

Un homme. Une destinée.

Ahead, a makeshift aperture embraced a crooked smile coated in dirt.

Malia led the procession to a halt and turned around.

"This is off the beaten path. History encapsulated within this place few had reached."

She turned again and lowered her profile, her hands finding the rugged sides of the improvised access, driving her people forward. Tallies and otherworldly symbols appeared on the bedrock, shouting stories that craved to be explored, ventured into. Malia smiled in the shadows of her light, looking at the strange writings with a certain disdain.

The procession narrowed down to one file, as the pathway shrunk, and the ceiling vault grew more suffocating. The walls were now bare, telltale signs of an uncharted section that experienced only a handful of trespassers. Malia's stride was resolute, purposeful, her light feet rapidly sweeping the dirt in the cold and droning underground nexus.

Her thoughts raced against the quiet march.

10.

12.

15.

17.

"Here," she declared, coming to a full stop. Her delicate fingers reached inside her satchel; she retrieved a block of explosives, a dark pasty compound the size of two butter sticks. One of its sides glowed under her torchlight, coated with a gel-like substance.

Malia stuck the explosive onto the wall to her right, inserted a small flashing beacon into the block and continued forward, all without a spoken word. She repeated the same process three times, at half-mile intervals.

Ahead, a warmer breeze had escaped through a well of light etched into the ground beneath them.

The procession stopped. Malia resumed her dramatic monologue.

"Ironically, it's... some of the tunnels we walked collapsed, their foundations too weak to support the heavy structures above, causing entire homes to sink. Today, we'll reenact this slice of history but also expose the bones to the sun. And this well below, before us... It shoots to the surface. I know the physics doesn't compute, but certain things can't be explained."

She propped her torchlight against the wall to her right and laid flat to reach for steel bars that were bolted onto the well's curved sides. As she descended into the hole, gravity seemed to shift, in a vertigo-inducing motion. Malia was now climbing up to a bright sky, flocks of birds entering her vision field.

It was an overgrown garden, in the back of an abandoned Maison Bourgeois whose white bricks were draped in various shades of brown. There was no traffic around the lot, no signs of activity nor occupation.

Baba and Agda emerged from the strange well, followed by

the cultists. Tall grass concealed the group from the lot's outer perimeter, a dead end that housed abandoned structures. Malia fought her way through the crowded vegetation, to a forged iron gate, and crossed to the street.

As the mob began flooding the cobblestoned cul-de-sac, Malia reached for the contents of her bag, once more.

"Finally, all deemed worthy of survival by the Eye will start this cycle anew, free of the shackles imposed by the industrial powers and history makers. Go and burn the bodies of the cursed."

The cultists dispersed quietly, expressing no thoughts nor objections. Malia found a detonator switch mounted on a small black metallic box, one of a sleek glossy finish. She briefly glanced at *Baba* and Agda, giving glimpses of a wordless questioning, and pressed the switch.

Down below, the Earth shattered. A blast roared in the underground, sending feverish tremors felt underfoot.

Silence settled once more.

10.

12.

14.

19.

A mile down the street, crackles erupted like runaway fireworks. Warehouses and public infrastructures began sinking, precipitated into the destructive patterns of their failing foundations.

The entire neighborhood was being leveled in the hands of a goddess who held the key to prescience and foresight. Before her eyes, history had been rewritten, inked in raw dirt and invasive vines.

Malia looked up and smiled, bathing in the bright sun of a hot morning. She addressed her entourage, her eyes closed.

"*Baba*, is it time?"

"Yes, Malia. Two more strikes, west and southwest of the city. ETA five minutes."

25

THE ARDEN

A fishing boat bounced against the quiet turquoise waters of a massive bay, one trapped within a crescent-shaped collection of small islands. Riz Qurban stood like a figurehead on the bow, his rifle sweeping the shore that showcased its pearl-like white sands under his attentive eyes.

A body bag was tucked under a bench behind him. Ajab and his men sat, quiet, under the deck's Bimini. Fadhlan, Natuna's local physician, steered the boat with a solemn posture.

Exhaustion, sensed Riz.

Mankind was held hostage, suffering a strange affliction that progressed too fast to be counteracted. Riz wrestled with conflicting thoughts on the legitimacy of Malia's actions, his mind warping under the relentless pressure she exerted.

"*Lembaga*. The institute, or institution. That's what we call this island, the one your superiors provided access to," shouted Fadhlan. The boat began speeding, preparing to slice through the beach's virgin sands.

"It belonged to a cartel, or so the local stories tell. We never approached it."

Fadhlan's voice faded as he negotiated his boat's beaching. Riz grabbed a handlebar and lowered his profile. A voice came through his earpiece.

"All clear, boss."

He gave a thumbs up without looking over his shoulder and braced for impact.

The boat cut through the wet sands, bouncing off the surface before sinking in. Coming to an abrupt stop, the CIA field officers dismounted, spreading in a half-circle to sweep the neighboring jungle. Fadhlan and Ajab anchored the boat and lifted the body bag on a stretcher, their grimacing expressions following a set of footsteps drawn on the paradisiac coastline.

Ajab sought Riz's attention and nodded yes.

"Alright. Let's go." Riz's assertive tone rained down on the scorching sands. The group formed a single file, the two scientists struggling under the weight of their cargo, in the center of the formation.

"*Sampah*! It's heavy!" Fadhlan whispered.

They all advanced to a natural opening, one leading further into the mainland.

The passageway was a majestic tunnel whose boundaries were forged in lush greens and intertwined, tangled roots. A few sun rays beamed on a sparkling clay soil, as resilient portions of the sun's soul. The heat was still present yet less aggressive, lingering not in sharp bursts, but as a low, unrelenting *hum*. Birds sang to the beat of mating calls and hungry offsprings.

Ahead, a staircase carved in rock led to a massive windowless structure built from wood paneling and compressed earth. The entryway stood tall, framed in smooth steel. A keypad was mounted in lieu of the lock mechanism.

Riz repressed a cough, patted his chest, and raised his hand.

The unit came to a halt. Two of his men assisted the doctor and the scientist with laying their precious cargo. He keyed a combination of numbers.

Click.

Riz pushed the door pane inward and rushed into the space, his rifle elegantly trained on the walls and lab instruments he found. Fadhlan and Ajab remained outside, guarding their load, while the others assisted their leader with the clearing.

Inside, a massive space housed a decontamination chamber, an autopsy room, cold storage, and scientific equipment.

"Clear!" shouted Riz, gauging the scale of the lab with pensive eyes. "From what management told me, the equipment here is still operational. You may need to recalibrate. Get to work."

The body bag was brought in and laid on the stainless steel of an autopsy table after a thorough cleaning. Ajab and Fadhlan oversaw a sequential decontamination for all personnel and items, running against the backdrop of a ticking clock, a relentless shadow that had engaged in the pursuit of mankind.

"This structure, the outer walls... It's bamboo judging by the scent and grain. What if the region were targeted?" asked Riz, addressing Ajab.

The environmental scientist raised brows. "The reports and the intel are conflicting. It seems *dead* carbon-based matter, one deprived of functional roots, is also left untouched by Malia's ordnances. But there are documented instances where 'natural' construction materials were consumed and transformed. I can't say for certain. Too many variables when it pertains to photosynthesis. It's environmental, so it cannot be replicated within the same parameters every iteration. And with the lack of time series data, collected or recorded as intervals over a period of time... we have to work around the clock. Fast."

Ajab's immutable eyes had transformed into something

more fleeting. A heavy blend of emotion and exhaustion permeated the space.

Hope eroded under Malia's powerful influence and terrorizing presence.

"Please do. Let's not forget what's at stake, Ajab. You can weigh the potential implications later."

The environmental scientist nodded yes and invited Riz to review Fadhlan's findings with him. Soon, the three stood over a pale corpse glowing in shades of gray. They wished to make it talk again.

26

YOU SHALL LOVE PEACE AS A MEANS TO NEW WARS

It was magic coursing through them.

Or perhaps, unexplainable bouts of chemistry, or rather twisted physics?

The sisterhood from Myanmar had somehow traveled back to Kabul, defying the new patterns of a world that gradually rejected modern technology.

They stood before Ramza, the latter attired in a diamond-covered tunic, sitting on a high throne of dramatic perspectives. The underground was warm, producing whiffs of floral scents that softened the ancient stones carvings found on the walls.

"Sisters. The travelers must account for the ferryman, surely?"

The ladies, all draped in green robes sparkling with golden specks, laid heavy eyes on the cult leader, unafraid to look up. There was defiance in their forward stance, in the open arms that betrayed no fear, no defensiveness nor coping mechanisms.

The youngest sister, the leading figure who primed the detonation in Myanmar with unwavering faith spoke.

"Ahriman has diluted our pure teachings, Ramza. You have entered the lower nature of men. Using parables to discharge yourself of your responsibilities. You've turned political, your unwarranted slaughtering hard proof of evil intents. We agreed to kill to serve a better creation, not to fulfill selfish needs. Remember. We do not run this world, we aid it."

Ramza carefully considered the speech for a few seconds, looking down on the small crowd. He raised his hand, and their attentive eyes froze.

Mannequins, stone figures, targets whose fears had been encapsulated in a glass dome.

Ramza descended on the sisters and weaved through the frozen crowd. He was surrounded by paralyzed bodies and torpefied faces, disabled pieces unable to contest his presence amongst them.

He spoke, his eyes darting between each sister.

"Six blind men and an elephant stood, each clutching a piece, each convinced of his truth. They quarreled over shadows, sightless to the whole—a debate without end. 'Is it a democracy?' one asked. 'An empire?' mused another. 'Or perhaps a dream spun from threads of socialism?' The elephant remained silent, for wisdom is patient. 'Will you offer your heart?' whispered the wind. 'Or does your sacrifice come with strings?'"

He studied the sisters. Thoughts ran amok as he weighed the pros and cons of their argument, the extent of their reach. Ahriman and Ahura Mazda, deities that birthed his cult following, had been good to him. And the powers he was bestowed upon, the strong mythos, the miracles... he truly *believed*.

But Ramza's actions suggested something more radical. A haunting ideology.

Power in capital.
Technocrats. Order. Structurally sound.
The name I wore. My legacy.
The name.

Ramza looked around for a few seconds, surveying the features he had grown accustomed to, and zoned out again. He raised his hands.

The bodies remained still, immortalized in a loud silence. In a strange juxtaposition, the eyes and mouths broke free.

"In childhood you are playful, in youth you are lustful, in old age you are feeble. So, when will you before my name be worshipful?"

The youngest sister's eyes quickly shifted, looking for Ramza in her peripheral vision. He kept away a few feet behind. Her eyes stilled. She spoke.

"You know we have rules, Ramza. There's no killing allowed among the Order members. We do intend to honor your name, and the bloodline it has birthed. But you've lost sight of our true purpose. We promised to honor Ahura's wishes, and so did your ancestors. She spoke to me, as you recall. What did she say?"

Ramza drank the words, waving his hands around like an orchestra conductor. His eyes were closed, turned toward the high ceiling.

He answered, "Well. That a mortal will bring her gifts upon Earth. A rebirth that would address the lower nature of Men. But beliefs alone do not bear enough weight in this physical plane. The gods need *men*. The prophecies require tangible actions. We need structure and control. We need movement, rather than a covert esoterism."

The sisters kept silent. Their faces closed inward with indignation.

Ramza refused to let the silence settle.

"Inaction. Betting all of your chips on a single, ambiguous faith with all these... Ramifications. There's no actionable... I can't support catering to the chaotic facet of a directionless campaign. You may go."

He raised his hand once more. The sisters stumbled and

collapsed, first unable to move the lower parts of their covered body.

Ramza mimicked a pounding motion with his right hand; the sisterhood found stronger footing and regained their bearings. The youngest led her group to a well of light cut through the bedrock facing the throne. They ignored Ramza in their exit, evading his vicious gaze.

Outside, the air was heavy, charged with an uncomfortable dampness. Leaves weaved through a tapestry of growing roots, moss, and tall grass.

The youngest sister stopped a few feet from the mausoleum's entrance and let her tired gaze lay on mountain ranges that sat in the prepossessing sight of a new world.

"Before we gather our followers, before we march against him... We must find a new designation, a new call name. An ode to our creators, our prophets. The emphasis on the resilient bond that is our sisterhood. Something bright in its darkness. *The Night Sisters of Ramza.*"

The others' ethereal eyes *widened* at the last words. One of the elders approached.

"Another vision?"

The youngest sister nodded *yes*, her eyes lost in the snowy peaks she watched crumble. She was contemplating; the latest developments had shown her that most individuals made of flesh were incapable of selfless service. For centuries, ideologies had been instrumentalized to serve its preachers, vocal crooks self-appointed as prophets. Their minds were poisoned by worldly aspirations: wealth, power, political capital, the call of the flesh... the youngest sister strongly believed herself to be righteous, however.

She had participated in a genocide, in unfathomable crimes against humanity, leaving mankind with no alternative options, effectively killing the very notion of free will.

But she was also given the keys to a technology, one she let Malia endorse publicly: a destroyer of worlds that was mentioned in the ancient writings of her theologies.

The one and true key to salvation.

"Yes. A body of water whose surface was fog. A clanking noise, wild patterns of sounds, like a cacophony of metals. And there, at the edge of a waterfall, I scream as the sound grows closer. The sequence of events repeats three times, until I jump. And then, the quiet."

The elder's face froze, her eyes seeking something in the dotted skies.

She replied, "Night Sisters."

27

ROUND THE PIGS

LANGLEY – VIRGINIA

The world was coming to an end. Technology had succumbed to its volatile nature. Analysts and strategists felt muted, distrustful of their tools.

The CIA was a writer who no longer knew how to construct effective propositions; the most powerful intelligence agency in the world had fallen, bursting apart in metaphorical strings of uncertainties, internalized fears, conflicts, and desertions.

Kia Lowes felt powerless. The shadow networks, the complex models, a rigorous training, *Analog*—all systems failed before her eyes. Her offices emptied in haste, the personnel fleeing to witness an incoming cataclysmic event with their loved ones, while the most persistent went into hiding.

A few had stayed. Whether patriots or completionists, they were pulled by a thread that offered the seductive prospect of survival. They *believed.*

Upper management also resisted the exodus, to Kia's surprise. But hallway rumors mentioned contingencies for the big wigs to find refuge underground.

A preservation of tactical assets, the whispers called it.

Amidst the chaos and the uncharted ventures, Miss Lowes clung to one focal point: Qurban. An old underground cable network brought the news earlier on: Qurban's team was thinning, but a local physician guided them to the infrastructure she had mapped out for *Analog*. Ajab expressed the possibility of developing a countermeasure to the new environmental parameters Malia triggered. Other conventional forces were either focused on crowd control, or lay defeated in the wake of the devastating attacks this Earth was enduring.

Her pet project, though struck by tragic losses and setbacks, was the closest to a viable solution and resolution.

She pushed forward, attempting to dismiss the thoughts as she purposefully walked toward a set of massive black doors. In her crowded mind, her children pleaded not to open them—to leave the building immediately and surrender to Malia's might.

The invisible thread guiding her to the conference room was strong, though; it was a composite of various *commitments*, intertwined with hopeful *prospects*. It tensed as she approached —billions of microscopic strings strummed to release whispers from the actors in her life.

Miss Lowes, Ajab made it.

"For Trey, Charles, and Miss Lovejoy yes. They agreed to follow us."

You are an ant. Look up as I hammer.

This could turn the tides of the war.

The surface is treacherous, villainous snakes feasting on rampant confusion.

Her hands found the door handle, a brief touch that silenced the voices.

Inside, proposals and rebuttals sparked in the air like deadly conjurations. Frustrations manifested through the cracks in the voices, like a flood of light no barrier could impede.

Kia's arrival trapped the fluttering noise in an imaginary box. President Hardwick was broadcast on a screen mounted across from the massive table she laid fingers on.

"I appreciate your support, ladies and gentlemen. I understand things may look a bit grim, but we have made a commitment, and I intend to follow through. President Hardwick."

Kia Lowes sought the President's attention. She was answering requests from an army of personal assistants buzzing around in a neutral-toned space that appeared to be a brutalist architectural exercise.

"Miss Lowes. Admirable. I tried to remain with you all, but some power players disagreed and took me by force. Some nonsense about being essential personnel. More like their flagship pawn. How do you all fare above?"

The blunt tone took her audience by surprise. Kia's face remained unphased by the bold approach. She knew Hardwick's psychological profile by heart and had followed her rise within the U.S. political echelons. This POTUS was unconventional. Balanced. Canvassing underserved communities. At odds with most lobbyists.

Kia genuinely believed she had been taken underground against her will.

"Madame President. It's a bit hectic here."

Kia's statement received verbal approval from the committee.

She resumed. "Naturally. And I'd like to thank the national security committee for their presence here today, their resilience. Their support has been invaluable, regardless of the outcome. On that note, Madame President, I may have good news for you. But this is more about adaptability to the new conditions that were introduced by our person of interest's organization, rather than a proper countermeasure."

The President waved her personnel away and approached the camera.

"Have you found a way to reverse *it* or prevent it?"

Kia nodded *no*. "Malia's attacks were meticulously planned, executed with the assistance of well-integrated actors. Aside from considerable financial resources, north of fifty billion dollars, she had the support of a shadow network with an unprecedented reach. Something no intelligence agency was prepared for. Sleeping agents, dormant cells, entire population centers loyal to one, single ideology with countless roots. Fortunately, we haven't found any trace of corruption in our own bodies but there could still be a leak somewhere else. In short, we can't prevent those attacks. Two hours ago, an offshore rig was consumed by one of her ordinances, a hundred miles away from Southeast Hampton. It's coming."

"What is this good news, then?"

"*Analog* has found a way to withstand the new conditions on the surface. We may be able to survive and rebuild, provided they make it back home."

The President and the National Security Committee were glued to her lips.

The former inquired, "Care to elaborate?"

"Yes, Madame President. Badeed Ajab, an environmental scientist working with Riz Qurban shared his findings regarding the body of a young male they found in Indonesia, one of Malia's *sicarios*. The one we discussed yesterday. The subject presented slight mutations in his respiratory systems, something induced by a chemical compound. We were able to isolate it."

She paused, surveying the room. The faces were stone-like, funambulists stepping on a delicate tightrope.

"Their location hasn't been compromised yet. If we can grant them safe passage to the States, *this* may be the key to our survival. Future wombs would birth babies that can thrive without the use of this controlled substance. Evolutionary theory. And since you already have an evacuation protocol in place, this would make for an effective counter-offensive."

Silence settled. Hardwick stared into the camera lens, her eyes direct and present.

"I assume you already devised a plan for transport?"

"Yes, Madame President. We found a corridor that was untouched by Malia's forever chemicals."

The President remained quiet, jotting down a few notes on a legal pad. She looked around the room, through the screen, and asked, "Any objections?"

The committee answered *no* in unison.

"Fine, Miss Lowes. Bring them home. I want to see you all downstairs before we lose contact. If it's not feasible, make sure you have oxygen reserves and find a safe spot. I am grateful for you all."

The feed cut to black, leaving only the heavy scent of a creeping fear.

SAGAPONACK — NY

Frictionless. Emphasis on wellness. Community oriented. Organic. Stimulating.

Those were the wishes expressed by the Fuggers in the ninetics, as they injected ghost funds into a top-secret doomsday bunker buried beneath the Hamptons.

Today, the culmination of a thirty-year construction project spread its feathers before its new residents. It was the first wonder of the new world, a sprawling underground city whose organic architecture borrowed from the late Frank Lloyd Wright. There was a notion of verticality introduced in the giant cave whose bedrock extended far beyond the stacked terraces.

The patriarch had led his tribe to the Garden of Eden, a layered jungle divided into sectors connected by a well-thought-out grid. Bamboo palms and morning glory danced on wood paneling and shatter-proof glass panes, elegantly spilling over ancient-looking cobblestoned streets flanked by a quiet monorail.

The air was pure, the water crisp, the locally grown foods nutritious and flavorful.

It was a wrinkle in time, a vestige of our past that bore foreshadowing lessons.

The patriarch stood there, on the lower levels, admiring a labor of love only the longstanding wealth of visionaries could afford. Around, members of the family went on about their day, shopping, strategizing for a hypothetical return to the surface, or furthering their knowledge base. A parallel economy was born in the wake of the *Great Exodus*; additional personnel were given safe asylum, housing and permanent benefits in exchange for their services, their expertise. Professors, engineers, designers, performing artists, psychiatrists, clinicians, janitors, and other essential assets were all willing to serve, complying for a shot at survival amongst members of the ruling class.

The Fuggers patriarch, the bonding compound of this enterprise, had achieved a sustainable model, an immutable balance.

A young teenage girl appeared in the backdrop, joyfully skipping toward him. She grabbed his hand and took in breathtaking views of the colony.

"Melinda. How are we doing today?" the man asked, with the gentleness of a trustworthy father.

"Great, Dad. Mr. Lonkins is peak education. Filtration systems? Groundbreaking."

The two laughed. The patriarch's smile starkly contrasted with his sad eyes. There were conflicting displays of his otherwise sharp features, like the implicit clues of a secret war.

He stared at his daughter, bathing in her joy, memorizing the quirks of her freckled face, the perfect teeth that did not quite fit within her juvenile outline.

She was an advanced student, a fun teen, yet a patient soul.

I hope you'll understand.

He gently pulled her toward an adjacent street with modern A-frame homes that served as storefronts. It had a charming European appeal to it, intimate alleys and detours that borrowed from Paris or South Manhattan's wilder grid. Foot traffic was light, and floral scents flooded the summer maze, complementing each click of the heels and loafers.

"There!" the daughter shouted, pointing at a coffee brown façade. A sign posted by the door read *Rome is open. First editions catalogue available upon request.*

It was her favorite place, the father knew, her refuge. She would order whispering wildflowers tea or hot chocolate and carefully browse the aisles of the massive two-story bookstore.

Here, books were preserved treasures from the surface, contemporaries and classics displayed in a beautiful cozy setting that favored reading. It was a magical library that also offered local delicacies to support a growing need for escapism.

While wars and struggles rocked the surface in waves of mass murder, the elite would enjoy a French-pressed coffee and a good book, in this subterranean paradise of theirs.

The patriarch followed his daughter down an aisle of nonfiction books, essays on intersectionality in feminism. She was reading summaries, exploring the depths of her potential next obsession. The father cast furtive glances at the neighboring sections—the bookstore, doubling as a coffee shop, was deserted, aside from the few staff gathered by the entrance.

In his mind, blood-curdling thoughts warmed up to a simmer.

I'm sorry.

Forgive me.

For I entered a path of redemption. For I will burn in the purifying fires of the Lord.

I ask that you protect her soul, and mine, as we embrace the consequences for the riches we lifted.

The signs of the end of times. Wars, conflicts, increasing levels of evil and wickedness in the world, rising environmental hazards, the emergence of a global economy. Most of which... we caused.

The simmer was brought to a boil.

At this very moment, as he embraced a form of spirituality he was never known for, the patriarch placed his hands on her jaw and neck lines.

And snapped her quiet.

"The body?"

"There."

Ajab pointed to a body bag with a ventilation circuit accented by its glossy surface.

A massive military plane loomed over the bag's polyester laminate. Further up its open ramp, beyond the access boundaries, Riz Qurban's men were patiently waiting, seated in worn leather pads bolted to the plane's frame.

"You're flying this thing?" asked Ajab. Wrinkles formed between his brows. He gripped the briefcase he was chained to even tighter.

"Yes. I was trained for this eventuality. We all were."

Qurban headed toward the bay, high knees climbing on the access ramp as he pulled the body bag up with Ajab; they dropped it in a receptacle carved into the cold, metal floor.

Riz stopped by his men. "This is it, ladies. We bring Ajab's compound home safely and find shelter. I'll need a control for my pre-flight checks. Given that... I will not be using autopilot."

One of the men nodded and walked to the cockpit. The others strapped up.

Down the ramp, Fadhlan's frame appeared, peeking. Ajab readjusted his glasses. Qurban smiled at the non-verbal tic.

"Fadhlan. Thank you for your assistance. Truly."

Riz coughed into his sleeve. Outside, the winds howled louder, massive banana leaves swaying alongside the runway's irregular edges.

"We have room, Doctor."

The local physician laughed at the suggestion. He replied, "No. This region has been untouched, and I believe it's good omens. Plus, I would rather die with my people, finding comfort in them. Safe flight. See it through."

Riz nodded in affirmation and flipped a nearby switch. Soon, the cargo bay plunged into the dark, red lights beaming on shadowy figures.

Riz checked his men's parachutes and ran stress tests on their automated deployment systems. The last *beep* marked the beginning of the next phase.

"Ajab, sit there, between them. Your cargo will be safer in this vacant spot. Least likely to be damaged in the event of a crash."

The environmental scientist obliged and sat, dropping the briefcase between his slender legs.

Riz joined his colleague in the cockpit and proceeded to conduct his checks.

As the switches finally lit up the cabin, he punched the thrusters to his right. The plane shook, its suspensions bouncing on the dirt road, the frame possessed by billions of loud convulsions. Riz surveyed the tree tops ahead, dense greenery crowning a dark volcano that extended to the clouds.

The plane lifted, its angle shifting against the ongoing winds.

"Take-off complete. Let's readjust. Make sure ACARS masking is in full effect. I rather not experience another crash."

SAGAPONACK — NY

He had crashed out. His mind had been thrown on a collision path, thrusted forward by sadness and guilt. His daughter's lifeless body still rested in his arms, in a quiet place no one interfered with.

The patriarch let go and headed for another aisle. He found the colorful spine of a thick hardcover book. The title read *America is a Zoo.*

Fascinating—how a single, well-articulated idea can wipe out worlds, he thought. His shaky hands pulled the book off the shelf and pressed against the wood beyond.

Click. A hidden compartment housed two handguns and four magazines. He retrieved it from the false panel and seized hold of a small radio clipped to his belt.

"Sec?"

"Post 1. Here."

"Residential. Here."

"Learning. Here."

"Location? Just checking."

"Post 1. MLK and Crescent."

"Residential. Six Magnolia Ct."

"Learning. The Persian Institute."

He replied, "Great. Standby."

The patriarch memorized the locations and drew a mental map. He needed to avoid those checkpoints; weapons had been banned from civilian use in the underground, but security was allowed to carry and operate small arms. Many objected, but the patriarch had stated—on many occasions—that he fully trusted his security detail, men who became family against the tumultuous backdrop of decades of faithful service.

What he omitted to mention is that he had a private cache.

And an obsession: the cleansing of generational colonizers. Old and modern slave runners. A ticket to heaven.

Redemption.

He tucked one of the guns in his black slacks and cocked the other one back.

Seventeen plus one in the chamber. Four magazines.

Seventy-two rounds. Seventy-one.

"Help!" he shouted, drawing the two on-site librarians closer.

Two shots rang. They fell like flies as they barely registered the gun in his hand. He dragged the bodies to where her daughter's lay and piled them together.

The door locked and a *Closed* sign bounced on the glass pane as he departed from the literary wonderland to spill out onto the cobblestones. A couple entered the street through a set of stairs cascading from a neighboring alleyway. They smiled at the patriarch, his handgun concealed behind his striped shirt. He approached them and gunned them down, their flesh hitting the stones with a deep bass.

He continued down a twisty pathway, entering and leaving shops and workspaces *changed.*

The city's artificial lighting grid dimmed. The body counts increased.

62.

The man had mapped out his tragic progression, using unknown routes left out of the original blueprints. More shots rang in the residential areas, impacts snatching lives from breached glass panes and splintered wood paneling.

68.

A siren thundered in the background, but he had isolated the sound and engaged with his eyesight. A child crossed a manicured lawn to his right. The young preppy boy drowned in tears, streaks of blood running down his face.

I forgot Henry.

The boy's small frame folded under the impact of a hollow tip bullet.

69.

Screams echoed from afar.

The patriarch soon entered a marvel of tropical brutalism that housed colorful art pieces and homey rugs. Lush indoor plants bound the ensemble with easy-on-the-eye patterns and soothing undertones.

"Zoya?"

A chime washed the exquisite interior.

"Administrator?"

The patriarch burst into tears, praying to the invisible skies, letting a deep sorrow invade his soul. The virtual assistant was quiet.

"Please disregard next command," he sobbed.

The AI remained quiet.

"And after my skin has been destroyed, yet in my flesh I will see God. For he has been patient with the transgressions of my person, the curse of my bloodline. For I accept that I have profited from misery, displacement, and hope. For I actively tend to the hurt souls I led. Father, forgive me."

The man's sobbing prevented the silence from settling. Time elapsed while he embraced the pain in his heart, the pounding in his fragmented mind, the tiredness of his stretched flesh.

"Zoya? Activate a protocol."

"Designation, Administrator?"

The man struggled to produce an answer. He took a deep breath and replied, "Klimt's *Death and Life.*"

"This is irreversible. Confirming?"

"Confirming, yes."

Within a wide range of enclosed units and open spaces, the

air was suddenly stripped of its oxygen. A form of anoxic treatment, a discreet engineer had explained to him. The Fuggers patriarch smiled and lay on the hardwood floor.

Specks appeared in his sight, a growing darkness filtering the noise out.

The man surrendered his life, content, as his world slipped away.

A LIFE-GIVING DEATH

The West was falling, engulfed with the flames of a cataclysmic force—*Malia*.

Her intricate network, a complex web of politicians, soldiers, craftsmen, and esoteric figures had subjected the world to their will. *They* engineered a precise sequence of events that promised to lure intelligence agencies into the darkest corners of their nightmarish fears: the death of technology, the vanishing of modern solutions.

From Ramza's strange aptitudes and shadow networks to the lethal efficiency of Agda and *Baba*'s wise counsel, all circumstances for the shaping of a new age were met.

In New York City, angels had gone rogue. Masses of individuals had fled westbound, chasing the futile hope of escaping an inexorable fate. Bodies dropped from the reflective façades of high castles, brain matter expanding outward in abstract compositions. Violent looting swept the city, animals in human form consumed by the wants of things that might never re-emerge.

A few souls had given up, the fragile shells of company men bursting from *within*, Evil incentivized with the new prospects sparked by Malia's intervention. They had surrendered to lust or drug use, finding escapism in self-destructive patterns. The plague descending from offshore dominoed to a beautiful chaos, a painting of infinite layers where minds collided in wild trajectories.

"From our poppy fields to crashing the den of the vile. Can we count this as a success, *Baba*?" Malia asked, her hands tightly wrapped around the yoke. The cockpit view gave to a bloated sky inhabited by thundering rain.

Baba gazed beyond his vision field, his puffy eyes and deep wrinkles testifying to time.

"Hm. Define success," he retorted.

The two remained silent, as Malia negotiated a turbulence. The plane carried a new wave of disciples. They were the last batch, the final froth of battered eyes that would convert the western territories and actively shape the *grand finale*. Agda had armed them with assault rifles, carefully watching over his human cattle in the cargo bay.

The C-130 initiated its descent. In the cockpit, the dark clouds cleared to reveal foggy shapes, blurred outlines of undulating structures and warm lights.

"Pulling thrusters, *Baba*. Going to time this precisely."

Malia reduced their speed, sinking into her seat, and pushed the intercom.

"Agda, we're landing."

She did not wait for a response and refocused on her instruments. The massive plane now flirted with a vast body of water, its dissipation trail parting the sea as it inched ever closer to the surface.

Foaming waves appeared before Malia's fiery eyes, crashing a massive plot of sand.

There lay a freakish spectacle—a strobing Ferris wheel, the tentacular tracks of an old rollercoaster, dancing lights—a lost kingdom from a long-forgotten golden age.

Coney Island.

"Down to one ten knots. Veering."

Malia led the C-130 to curve right, parallel to the beach line; the waves became closing walls, imperturbably looping in unpredictable fluctuations.

"Air brakes."

Baba obliged and suddenly, the plane slowed against the friction of an elastic layer, one invisible to the naked eye. It lowered closer to the ground, the landing gear still stowed within its wheeling well.

Instruments began to ring.

"Shutting TAWS."

A heavy silence settled, the tremors of the cabin a chilling warning.

"Impact," continued Malia, her voice steady and measured.

The plane breached the spume, carving deeper into the soft sands below. It drifted briefly toward the ocean, quickly correcting its course as its frame shrieked against the beach's sea stacks.

An eerie quiet blanketed the inside. None of the parties involved betrayed fear, nor did they produce the slightest sound. Malia was smiling, her eyes lost in the rising tides to her right.

"*Agda*, go hunt. Release them," she shouted.

In the cargo bay, Agda forced the ramp open. The disciples poured onto the beach, a swarming mass shifting toward the nearby cityscape like a biblical plague. He followed behind, his face held high toward the skies, the frame of his exoskeleton casting a wide, imposing shadow over the skyline.

Malia and *Baba* set foot on the empty shore as well, high knees working against the rip currents. As their footprints settled toward the amusement park before them, black dust rose from the deep sea, swirling up and blowing forward. A metallic pitter-patter exercised dominance over the waves' rumble and grew closer.

And closer.

Malia and *Baba* halted their course, inhaling the salty ocean breeze. The black powder consumed the plane that now towered over them, its metal panes and complex circuits melting into the Atlantic.

Soon, it was gone, like the ghost of a past scene, in a distant timeline.

As Malia's engineered *monster* reached for New York City, she sought *Baba*'s attention.

"How did we fare?" she asked.

He turned and stared into the ocean.

"What of the hourglass that has been turned? Only time will tell."

FOREIGN AGENT

NYC — NEW VIRGIN TERRITORIES

"Mr. Qurban? I think anonymity and confidentiality are irrelevant at this point. How do you feel?" Ajab asked against the backdrop of a quiet glider plane, his voice a muffled drum trapped within a breathing apparatus.

The clearing they stood in was carpeted with soft grass glowing in translucent shades of green, vines intertwined with thorned roses within its close perimeter. Riz Qurban's hidden sickness seethed to break free. His skin was pale, scaled in shades of gray, an unhealthy shine flooding his clear mask.

Beneath his feet, a crack in the dark soil revealed a trail leading to a natural body of water.

"Mr. Qurban?"

"Yes."

"How do you feel?"

"I'm ready to close this chapter, Ajab. With or without our samples. Pray those new rifles hold."

A silence settled between the team members. Riz's men quietly gathered around their leader; there was an unspoken truth, the common knowledge that discussing diseases risked dulling the men's edges, effectively disrupting their advance.

Ajab held onto his briefcase firmly, acknowledging Riz's remark with a nod. He looked at the scorching sun and frowned. Further down, beyond the pond, something *slithered* under a rich canopy. Riz approached the cracked trail and signaled for his men to follow.

The things. Plural. A series of waves shook the body of leaves ahead, once more.

His finger grazed the rifle's trigger. Its iridescent coating cleverly shielded the weapon from both the harsh sun and Malia's destructive touch.

The invisible pack the group had sensed flashed through the green layers before them, unseen yet unaware. Soon, the jungle's backdrop reclaimed its throne.

Riz shushed his men with a finger to his mask's filter. They advanced, silently breaching the natural pool that glistened before their widening eyes, while their idle hands marveled at the clear water.

Riz lowered his profile, an electrical fire tearing through his bones. Pain was now a recurring pattern, a pulse that re-emerged from the depths of his soul. His team followed suit, all blending in with the buffer zone between air and water.

They remained there for a few minutes, listening to the wilderness, picking apart various sets of sounds. Thoughts began flowing uncontrollably through Riz's crowded mind.

Kia's shelter is two miles northbound. Sixteen dependents. Thirty-three high ranking officials.

Life expectancy, Mr. Qurban? Pick a number.

It's a psychological process similar to palliative care. You progressively withdraw from moral considerations. You become a wild card.

A Joker?

Precisely.

"Ok, we're clear to proceed. Shelter is two miles northbound. We need to move fast."

Riz continued forward, rising from the waters like an undead. Beyond the pool, a rocky slide descended into a trail that was flanked by overgrown elephant ears. The men walked the path, dissociating the light drag of the surrounding vegetation with more concerning sounds.

Each step brought Ajab closer to a resolution. He had developed a basic protection against Malia's life-giving death kiss, but what rested in his blanched hand, however painful, could offer mankind a second chance. He carefully mapped his steps, scanning his surroundings.

At the trail's end stood an inground water tank, a stainless-steel cylinder nearly flushed with the lush soil that housed elderberry bushes and citrus saplings. The tank was nearly full, its murky water drawing the men's faces on its surface.

Riz surveyed their surroundings and identified a protrusion on the ground, a few feet from the tank. His light steps drove him to study the anomaly, a layer of banana leaves hell-bent on blurring its contours.

He swept them to reveal a hatch; the metal trap door was punctured by hundreds of small craters, like the marks of a percussion hammer.

Ajab turned back to the tank. "Noticed how the stainless steel was left unaltered? Something regarding association, affiliation with organic liquids, maybe matters."

Riz nodded yes quietly and spun the hatch's lock mechanism. It sprung open, giving views to a bottomless pit adorned with a metal ladder.

Somewhere in the vicinity, a shadow flew over the bordering tree lines. Weapons sought the foreign agent.

"Weapons down!" shouted Riz. He stood and scanned the perimeter. "The tally keeper? The soulless one?"

The others shifted their attention between their leader and the closing shadow. Ajab frowned and stepped back.

He appeared to them, his footprint soundless. A mountain of metal and gas. The mute grim reaper, compliant and relentless.

Agda.

Riz faced Malia's faithful killer, shielding his men from the tallies carved onto his exoskeleton suit.

The two remained silent, their eyes locked in a wordless conversation.

"Boss?" one of the CIA officers inquired.

Riz ignored the request and looked up to the skies. A tear rolled down his emaciated cheekbones, blurred by his fogging mask.

Withdrawing from moral considerations.

For I no longer belong to this Kingdom.

I see.

He sang, in a whisper.

"*Agda*, kill. Leave the briefcase bearer unharmed."

31

A THRONE OF SNAKES

NYC — NEW VIRGIN TERRITORIES — THIRTY MINUTES EARLIER

"I love you Trey," Kia whispered in a confiding mood. She had already kissed her husband goodbye, almost lost in his emerald-green eyes and rich, dark undertones. Finding comfort in her strong embrace, her daughter Trey melted into her crisp, floral fragrance.

Kia had found refuge in an unmapped bunker, grateful to have been granted asylum by her agency. Although no price was set, she hoped to repay the remnants of her nation, to reinstate a greater power, a people she regarded as true. A timeline bloomed in her brain, an ever-expanding stem with petals for the fragments of her life.

She raced her own dilemmas on the glassy surface of this dreamworld, dashing left and right, searching for answers within the depths of her memories.

A giant flip clock materialized above. The numbers ran wild and turned into words in red lettering.

NOW or never.

Kia snapped back as she let go of her daughter. Crossing the threshold of a concrete door frame, she engaged a narrow hallway that zigzagged and housed small living units, each door marking new boundaries.

Her thoughts meddled with the conversations echoing further ahead.

God, it's me. Please bring back Qurban alive.

It's no longer a war. They won.

The reconstruction effort? I concur. That's a better use of resources.

Where is the workforce? Any calls from the House?

It's the mobilization of human resources before anything else. And what if...

What if, Kia... what if this was a blessing in disguise?

"Kia."

President Hardwick stood in the hangar that appeared ahead, one that expanded upward to a soaring ceiling. Madame President was surrounded by familiar faces, most of which were shaded in salt and pepper grays, defined by deep wrinkles.

The President had been taken to this underground shelter due to its proximity to her most recent location, before the world no longer tolerated its parasitic guests. Her security detail partook in the exodus, first escorting her through a jungle of unparalleled density, where bird songs incited widespread fear and paranoia, and gun shots brought hope.

"Madame President."

The men and women gravitating around nodded at Kia, bags drooping under their sad eyes. Despair had left the room quiet, diminishing the militant spirit of those who once welcomed challenges.

Kia pursued, "We lost contact an hour ago, but our asset is due in twenty-five minutes."

President Hardwick's intense eyes shifted from Kia's intel to the installation's features. The ceilings consisted of exposed pipes and neatly grouped wires running to the intersecting walls. To her right, an arched doorway led to the sad shell of a testing facility, massive Xs drawn on the floor, arranged in a grid.

There, computers and older analog equipment were operated by a group of ten individuals discussing their specificities in an animated exchange.

"Let us pray." The President returned to Kia. "Miss Lowes, who do we have on site? And what is your take on the current developments. Most of us here are politicians, but overcoming this... It requires another set of skills."

Her cabinet members and advisors declined to object, still as the night.

Kia replied, "We have thirty individuals on site, including the ones in *this* space. Three civil engineers. Two chemists. Two biochemists. Six security personnel. Four intelligence officers. Five cabinet members. Eight civilians."

She paused at the last words, reflecting back upon the President's losses, her own family buried alive as their Victorian home sank. The news had traveled, somehow.

"At this stage, I'd recommend collecting as much data as possible and staying sheltered. The situation is complex, between Malia's current whereabouts, her organization's reach, and what the collapse of industrialized nations implies for us... we need to sort out the variables to get a clearer picture. Concurrently, or as a close second priority, is comms. Without some form of coordination, we'll face major overlaps. The sign—"

A loud and harsh buzz cut the ongoing discussions short. The President's security detail surged forward.

Kia raised her hand. "We have visitors." She waved at the engineers nearby. "Who is it?"

One of the brains rushed to a computer screen that shone *truth* on his pale skin.

He shouted, "Your assets. Two pax."

Kia and the President's entourage followed their protection detail into a wider hallway. Beyond the walkway, a massive, blast-rated bunker door dominated a concrete wall.

Kia approached the lock mechanisms and opened the access, anxious to welcome her assets home.

It was a sickly man she found at the door, the depleted shell of a weathered soul. The man accompanying him seemed possessed by microtremors, as if haunted by nightmarish visions. Blood splatters punctured his mask.

Kia asked, "Qurban? Ajab? Where are the others?"

He looked at her and produced a reserved smile, a benevolent gesture that warmed her heart. She had grown fond of the wise man who head speared her vision.

Riz seemed content, his aging face opening to her presence.

He spoke. "*Agda*. Spare her, and her bloodline."

An unforeseen shadow emerged from the access tunnel and breached the perimeter. Bullets rained down on the security detail, POTUS and her cabinet members, as well as the engineers, Agda's handgun rendered quiet by a sleek suppressor. His exoskeleton suit rejected the stray bullets that ricocheted on its beaten surface, its bearer responding with inevitability and authority. The bodies collapsed in sync, leaving Kia to process the massacre alone, as the hitman returned to her.

Seconds stretched, long bouts of struggles, cascading thoughts and shifty eyes.

Riz's understated smile settled on his face.

"Miss Lowes. Malia should be here shortly. Ajab, go sit."

The environmental scientist was still in shock, offering no response to the massacres he himself had also witnessed, both on the surface and underground. He complied and headed toward the computers room.

Kia's eyes welled up, fighting to stay their course, beaming at her asset. Agda left to venture into a nearby hallway. Her heart began pounding.

Riz raised his hand. "No, Kia. You're not losing them." He briefly paused, removing his mask. A dry cough rocked his airways. "Let's join Ajab."

Despite his deteriorating condition, his gun was steady, trained at a spot between her eyes.

Screams echoed from the nearby hallway. She turned and readied to run, until a warning shot froze her in place, its loud bass bouncing off the concrete.

"Join Ajab. This is my last warning, Kia. *Agda* knows how to spread *fear*. But he won't hurt them unless I tell him to."

She obliged, seeking clarification in his tired eyes. They sat across from Ajab, who had opened the briefcase he was chained to and unlocked his cuff, like a diamond courier under duress.

Riz peered beyond the table they had found, casual in his handling of the situation.

"Aside from your family members, Kia, there's no one else left."

A couple of rogue shots rang afar. Kia jolted.

"I want you to listen carefully and forgo any moral considerations. We are on a tight schedule." His words struck with authority, though his eyes betrayed tears. "I run your person of interest's organization. My ancestors, the Durannis, have been... working on a countermeasure to effectively eliminate the corrupt powers of westernized dynasties. I've prepared for this eventuality. For years, faithfully serving the agency as a pawn, while forging alliances through Malia. My proxy."

He paused.

"My daughter."

Kia widened to the reveal, tears bursting out of control. There were maybe foreshadowing signs, breadcrumbs he had left to appease his inner voice, the guide to righteousness or wickedness. Maybe she had missed them, his loyal service an effective decoy deployed in many layers.

Riz disrupted her train of thoughts.

"There are many other details, riflemen, scored heists and magic. But most will trickle down eventually, provided you survive this next hour. I'm going to leave you with a choice, Kia."

He pulled Ajab's briefcase closer. His nonchalance was disarming, an offbeat performance to a pivotal point in history.

"You and Ajab will develop a better societal model for your people. We will grant you sizeable territories and a ceasefire will be enforced. Understand, you are given an opportunity to thrive without the... complicated people we've had to subject to. However, this is conditional to your obedience to Ramza's judgment—an individual you may encounter—and the forsaking of every other ideology. Only a cohesive body can properly harness the power of *that* which my daughter initiated. Do you understand what's at stake here? Not as mere points of contention, but as inevitable outcomes."

Kia dried her tears, his words like hot blades applied to a leaking wound. She fought to contain her racing heart, deeply broken by his betrayal.

"What if I refuse? How could you?"

Her voice shook.

"Kia, Kia. You may never understand what true conviction does for your soul. When you reach that stage, if you do, you'll find that there are no other moral considerations, no buyouts, no compromise. If you refuse, I will kill you both. I'll take no pleasure in cutting your lives short, so I will be humane in my methods."

He coughed, stepping away from the table. Kia reviewed the contents of Ajab's case; there were charts, diagrams, and long blocks of texts split in headings and subheadings. On the right, vials and samples were secured in shockproof foam.

Riz added, "My people won't need this. They are immune. And I'm dying."

He placed a hand on his chest and smiled.

"So... Kia? Naturally, Ajab already agreed. You bear the responsibility now."

Dying? Kia wondered. She stole a brief glance at a nearby hallway, hunting for sounds.

Trey.

Charles. The apple of my eye.

She turned back to Riz, searching for a spasm, a flutter, or the telltale signs of a break in character. The man was unmoved by her silent questioning, by the horrifying implications of his actions.

"I will."

Riz nodded in agreement.

"Reasonable. You've ta—" Footsteps clicked in deep notes.

Riz resumed, shouting, "Malia! The wound of the sword will heal, but not that of the tongue!"

The footfalls quieted down. Kia could not grasp this new reality. Was Malia aware of her dad's schemes? Will he survive this encounter? She could not get past the one he called Agda, regardless. *What* was he?

The steps resumed their advance.

Malia revealed herself, her aura dispensing fear that flooded Kia like a metastatic cancer.

She wore a tactical suit grazed by a fine layer of dust and pollen. Her dark yellow undertones were dipped in a golden coating, highlighting the rich black curls she wore shoulder length. In the light of past and recent developments, Kia had always failed to profile her: was she ruthless, mischievous, or abused?

The drug lord who claimed to have reshaped the world walked a careful stride, quiet and docile, her hazel eyes compliant to Riz's gaze.

She stopped a few feet shy from her biological father, her eyes soulless and malleable.

"Mr. Qurban?" she asked courteously.

"Riz. Now, feel the chains of your own thoughts dissolve as you sink deeper into my command. With each word I speak, your will bends. Merges with mine. As the next phrase echoes through your mind, you are bound to my will. Now, *awaken*."

Malia snapped out of her lost gaze, sizing Riz, studying Kia and Ajab with an indescribable kind of curiosity.

"Riz?"

He acknowledged the name with a nod and took a deep breath.

"That is right, Malia. Is *Baba* gone?"

She nodded yes. Riz took her in, wrapping his arms around her smaller frame in a fatherly embrace.

"Who?" she asked, still welcoming the gesture.

"Who am I? Remember the night you escaped with *Baba*, the drone strike that leveled your village? The caves?"

The graphic violence and the all-around chaos were imprinted in her brain, stubborn memories that starred hooded demons whose coal-black eyes petrified.

She replied gravely, "Yes."

"It was all part of the plan. Decoys deployed to draw in the U.S. coalition... doubling as a trick of the mind to propel you forward. Ramza knows. *Baba* knows. Malia. Understand. I am your biological father."

Her response to the confession proved odd, barren of concerns or astonishment; she simply burst into tears, sinking into his tall frame, accepting of the fate that had been manufactured for her. She declined to comment, joyful tears drowning her scarred face.

Kia and Ajab understood.

Hypnotic triggers. Advanced.

Riz whispered, both father and daughter privy to a secret, "I'm also dying daughter. From a sickness that was caused by the *abject* failures of our kind. This is your opportunity to avert further crises. The woman behind me, Kia Lowes, you will grant her U.S. territories to support our efforts. I owe her, so I salvaged a seat at the table. The gentleman, Ajab, is a floater. Use him as you see fit. Agda will also remain with you."

Malia's words were no longer striking when spoken, but soft and contained. Who was she, at the very core of her being? The answer lay in this newfound relationship, she thought. There, in this tragic conclusion, she no longer felt the need to question his motive.

"Will you stay with me, *Baba*?"

Riz smiled. "No, *gulaaba*. We all answer to higher powers. I will soon head for the surface, for I have sinned greatly, and made you sacrifice so much."

He gently rubbed her curls, protective of her person.

Kia was flooded with competing feelings as a firsthand witness. His sorrow and pain, his surrender, the logic that backed his reasoning. All almost... sound.

"I need to see my family," she said.

Riz released Malia and replied, "You may. The timeline is yours to define. Remember, Agda will always be there, lurking. He was cursed, and therefore will never die."

The implications of this threat were fear-inducing. She left the space with a cluttered mind and a pounding heart, sweat beads flowing on her beautiful dark skin.

Her stride expanded to a run, her shadow dancing on the nearby walls.

The monster.

He was there, towering over her loved ones, his impressive frame blocking the access. He swiftly turned.

"I was to—"

Before she could finish, the killing machine passed her, leaving the scene without a sound.

At the edge of a precipice, her thoughts shaped a feverish dream; in the coldness of this brutalist den, strong roots had outlived their fate, scarce yet rich in their composition.

She hugged her tribe, the anchors that withstood the madness.

32

HE WHO HAD MASTERED THE NIGHT

R iz Qurban rose from the underground, his eyes fixed on the full moon above.

The hissing of his oxygen tank matched the heavy drumming of his heart, left to thunder in the quiet night. He burst into tears, closing the hatch beneath.

"Ahriman. I have fulfilled your vision. Whispers to loud cry. And because my time nears its end, I will walk this Earth. And solve the last puzzle."

His voice was muffled, crackled. He began walking the virgin territories, the complicated jungle that once was New York City.

South to D.C.

Alongside the careful planning of his betrayal, Riz had memorized a great deal of information. Faces, places, political inclinations... all geared toward one purpose: to destroy and recreate anew.

"Will you protect my daughter? Where do you stand with *Baba?* Will Agda remain?"

He shouted into the night, walking a trail coated with short grass; tall bushes flanked his sides, providing a privacy screen for his self-talk. A stream flowed peacefully beyond the path's boundaries, somewhere to his right. He listened to the current for a moment, rejecting the heavy burden of his repressed emotions.

"I SAW that you were the only viable path, that Ahura's model was not sustainable. I made a choice, and you supplied me. Will I be invited to sit by your throne? To watch her grow. And... what of this new world? And Kia."

He reached the top of a gargantuan hill, a giant of floral whiffs overlooking an oasis that bloomed in concentric layers of greens.

The path down was steep. A fire burned slow within his moving corpse, cancerous lumps pressing on his tight flesh.

"I... I stopped taking the meds."

He began patting his back, awkwardly reaching for the backpack he carried. He found the tape handle and let go.

Malia, Agda. The supplier. The killer.

Baba. The wild card.

Kia. The collateral.

Ajab. The offset.

Vectors binding stars. The galaxy warping inward.

He paused the thoughts, regulating his breathing to combat a growing dizziness.

All siphoned away into the vacuum of the great destroyer. Ahriman.

As he resumed his long, arduous journey down to the majestic oasis, Riz burst into manic laughter. He had come to a strange realization: the age of spies and complicated agencies was over.

Before his eyes unfolded something more primal, almost magical. From the tradecraft to a global reset, from agents of influence to agents of gods, the world had assumed a different form. Under his guidance, the pawns of his board thrust forward, evading the grasp of other pieces.

He was the stunt, the claim, the muscles, the brain… he was all and nothing. Survival in sickness. Whispers and shouts. For he had assumed the position the gods had bestowed upon him.

He reached the bank, the moon a glowing circle distorted by the quiet ripples of dragonflies. His oxygen mask flashed in the night, reduced to a red light strobing in a fast sequence.

"I surrender."

Riz negotiated the embankment portion as it veered right, his footsteps sinking into fine, crystallized dirt, one sending sparkling reflections into his already altered vision. His fingers counted something beyond the tree lines, along his right flank.

"One last crop to weed out. A few more rotten roots."

He stopped and turned to the outer layers of greenery, his eyes streaks of reds in the darkness.

"There."

Beyond the citrus and peachy fragrances lay a ground hole, a natural well wide enough to accommodate a full-size adult. Riz kneeled and took his backpack off, his thoughts racing to a mad clock.

No, Kia. No outside influence. A clean slate on which you'll sketch your masterpiece. No fingers poking at your palette.

He looked down the hole and shouted, "Friendly!"

Below, a head emerged from a perpendicular conduit. The older man was pale as the moon, his skin torn by deep cuts that had just dried. He held a small oxygen mask to his face, the wires running wild to a tank clipped onto his soiled shirt.

His muffled voice inquired, "Yes?"

"Riz Qurban, CIA. I was tasked with recovering a certain John C. Haller, and the Alexandria think tank?"

The man's response sounded shaky, his voice outstretched in wild inflexions and pitches.

"This is him. Haller. I... we hid."

Riz interjected, "You are safe M. Haller. Is this well sealed? How many of you in there?"

John Haller scraped the curved sides of the well to pull himself up, frantic, eyes drowning in tears. He emerged to the surface, his hand applying pressure on a damaged oxygen breather that crackled. More survivors emerged behind him; their competing cries disrupted the oasis' equilibrium.

"I understand that this is quite traumatic, but I need you all to quiet down. Malia is searching for survivors."

And so was I.

"How many people, John?" Riz asked, once more. Bodies continued rising from the well.

John answered, tears singing through his tired voice.

"We're all here, f... five." He began shaking and sat to find balance in this world he no longer understood. The star lobbyist. The fixer. Washington D.C.'s grim reaper.

Riz nodded *yes.* "Good, John. Give me a few seconds, ok? Everybody else, please line up for ID."

The others followed, repressing violent tears that threatened to burst apart in sparkling fragments.

In a split second, Riz drew his coated handgun and fired.

A bullet for each soul. The falling bodies were soundless, overwhelmed by the thundering gunshots.

He dragged the bodies back to the well, fighting his achy muscles and swollen organs. One by one, they dropped, engulfed with the darkness of an improvised grave.

Some limbs twitched, nerves protesting the lack of response from the brain. Riz dug in his backpack and retrieved a small metal sphere. He twisted and pulled its pin, let go of its spoon; the grenade landed on their flesh, down in the well.

He ran back to the oasis, drawing one of his last breaths.

Behind, a massive explosion shook the ground, dirt raining down in a soothing clattering.

Lying by the bank, Riz waited for the detonation's echoes to fade.

As the silence settled, he retrieved a framed object from his bag, a picture. A toddler with an impressive thatch of curls latched onto a woman with beautiful eyes like pools of liquid gold. Riz ran his hand on the photograph, reminiscing.

"Bring the world to its knees, daughter."

He laid the frame down, retrieved his handgun and removed his mask.

The air was oppressive, pressing on his burning lungs. He held his breath and placed the barrel of his weapon against his temple.

Click.

The darkness boomed in.

Soon, Riz would become a lost ruin—the vestige of a mythos.

There, he had mastered the night.

33

THE HORSEMAN

"West. *Tez!*" shouted *Baba*. He led a group of followers through a shallow basin that stretched to the horizon, where a lavish sunset beamed its warmth.

Their steps were measured, calculated, muscles straining against the pull of a side current. None wore any protective equipment; they roamed free in this new world, unaware of their own limitations.

The faces were nondescript, devoid of tics and expressions; those figures of clay trailed *Baba*, poised to cleanse the Earth of mankind's invasive subsets.

Memories haunted him as he fought to conceal his pain.

The poppy fields.

My daughter. My protégé.

She was never given an alternative. A puppet whose mouth stretched.

He held onto a piece of fabric with a coarse thread and underlying gold accents. His fingers could still feel his god daughter's kisses applied on the edges, one of the few affectionate gestures she ever produced.

Malia was a child soldier, precipitated into war by abusive

patriarchs. *Baba* was one of them, and even though he had tried to offset the damage by empowering his student, the trauma ran too deep, the circumstances never-changing.

Between Ramza's spiritual false equivalence, Agda's murky loyalties, Qurban's manipulative nature, and the world's distasteful views on environmental policies, Malia was set for failure, serving shifty schemes.

And so is human nature. No amount of reset, extinction-level event—even spanning over centuries—could change our responses and stubborn aspirations. Those narcotics may rewire humanity, correct our course... but what if... what if someone poisons the well, once more?

They soon set foot on red clay, wet from the basin's spills. Further ahead, the nitrogen-rich soils shifted to darker green patches, their clovers and white flowers soft to the touch.

The clay became dirt, its characteristic reds turned into emeralds and citrine quartz.

There was a timid tree line to the left, with nascent palm trees that bordered another oasis.

Baba came to a halt, surveying the field that expanded for miles. It was rich, fertile, and leveled.

He turned to his cohort and ordered, "Start building."

34

THE HEIR

The voices in her head. They were gone. No more unsolicited advice for murderers. No more dark rooms filled with personifications.

Malia was free from her mental shackles, the memories of her biological father returned to her unscathed. *Baba* still mattered much, and anger rattled the cages of her compartmentalized thoughts all the same, but closure was a sweet friend and fine addition, a joyful disease stronger than any narcotics.

She was flying a wide body aircraft that had been outfitted with a special coating. One of her disciples handled the yoke in the co-pilot seat, stoic and unnaturally stiff.

How high, Malia thought.

The drug heiress, daughter of Riz Qurban, had decided to return to her kingdom. The Eye of Ramza was an asset she intended to leverage, and Kabul would become the political powerhouse of this brave new world.

But first, she needed to operate adjustments.

The plane landed on a dirt runway, weeds and natural

debris swept in ditches dug into its flanks. Malia had powered off all communications and geolocation systems in the region, risking her life to arrive undetected, assisted by a loyal follower who had submitted to her drugs.

"You," she demanded from her copilot. He turned to her in a mechanical motion.

"Yes, all seeing."

Malia retrieved a handgun from under her seat and pressed it against his forehead. He betrayed no response, no twitch.

The gun went off, brain matter splattering all over the cockpit. Malia's skin was now tainted with blood, streaks running across her devious smile.

"My father was a good man."

She cleaned up and headed for the cargo bay. A red box was mounted onto the wall to her right; she snatched it and flipped the locks open.

"Ok," she muttered to herself.

Incendiary grenades, coated in a glossy white. Malia threw one in the cockpit and another one in the bay, engaging the opening ramp that led to the runway.

Soon, the aircraft went up in bright white flames, vacuumed clean in broad daylight.

KABUL — AFGHANISTAN — AN HOUR LATER

Masses of cultists had swarmed the former city center. Reconstruction efforts were already ongoing; bamboo, ferrock, and clay shaped low structures and accessways. The integration was flawless, woven into the tapestry of the wild.

The crowds began converging toward Malia as she arrived, the narcotics coursing through their veins stimulating a response to her pheromones; it was a safeguard the Hourglass Network had devised in the utmost secrecy, a way to counteract Ramza's growing influence.

As they approached, she whispered, "Where is Ramza?"

Fingers pointed to a structure up a rolling hill, a single-block home built from light-shaded material. Malia smiled and waved her disciples away.

A few minutes later, her footprints sank into the wet soil of a steep driveway, each step accompanied by a barrage of thoughts.

A con artist profiting from faith. A tyrant.

"Powers" bestowed upon you that are nothing more than clever tricks and theatrics.

Your sisters bear the true power, and you turned on them.

Roaming the immediate perimeter, Malia spotted no guards, no disciples. The property was left *virgin*, in a silent agreement between the owner and his community.

An ego as big as his oversight.

She stepped to the woven jute entry, slid in quietly.

Inside, a massive room featured a sunken pit and light curtains that swayed under the outside breeze. Lying in the middle was Ramza, surrounded by a plethora of naked cultists, men and women who peacefully rested on a custom piece of fabric.

Ramza appeared more mundane under the daylight, his skin free of ceremonial makeup, eye shadow and complicated accessories. A smile played on his hawkish features, two women propped in his arms.

Malia surveyed the scene, praying.

May you find guidance. And fulfillment in serving others, rather than pandering to your own selfish desires.

In the delicate kiss of a summer breeze, her weapon found its mark—and took his life.

IRAN — FIVE MONTHS LATER

The sisterhood sought its inner light, bodies adrift in a state of meditation.

The *Night Sisters of Ramza* were headquartered in a secretive compound rebuilt on the steep side of a massive mountain range. Lush gardens obscured the views from neighboring trails, while the structures lay buried within thick canopies.

Beneath the sheltering shade of a giant sequoia, the sisters reflected upon their own aspirations, seeking the delicate tipping point between the flesh and the soul. With closed eyes, they saw more clearly than ever.

Footsteps echoed in their mind, a faint whisper that faded at times.

Their eyes opened.

"Agda," one of the sisters shared. They turned around and faced the quiet giant.

The one who spoke raised her hand; he bowed, sinking to his knees, blending with the earth.

"Reclaim your *voice*."

The last word was accompanied by a hand motion, a half-circle the lead sister drew above his bent frame. He collapsed, rattling against the hard ground, contorting in pain as muffled sounds attempted to break out from *within*.

The metal from his exoskeleton stilled. Agda was no longer in control, suffering an unforeseen metamorphosis. His eyes widened, his breath shallow. The exposed flesh on his partially covered face pulsed with protruding veins and broken blood vessels.

His hands fumbled for his mask, disoriented by the acute pain he was afflicted with.

The sisters watched in silent vigil, observing every struggle, monitoring every desperate attempt.

Finally, he managed to get a grasp, effectively removing the device his skin had been paired with throughout his adult life. Routine maintenance on the device had averted infections and organic fusion with his tissue, but the separation still brought searing pain, a piece of his identity surrendered to a new reality.

The world tasted bitter, with a soupçon of heaviness in the atmosphere that could not quite be associated with humidity or other known phenomena.

His lungs adjusted, and with a forceful exhale, he expelled calcified foreign matter.

"Let it out," the lead sister urged.

Agda vomited his pain, purging his body of a dark matter that now felt unwelcome.

"We are lifting this curse, Agda. Forgive us for being accomplices in the wasting of your early years."

Agda's eyes danced against the sisters. He rose to his knees once more.

His lips trembled under the realization that he was no longer bound to his executioner role.

There, he asked, "What... of me?"

Q: There is a strong environmentalist angle in this novel. You've never done this before as an author. What prompted you to?

A: Great question. I've always challenged myself with every project—not just in terms of size, scope, scale, or budget, but also in crossing genres and themes and breaking patterns. There's always been a special place in my heart for environmental challenges.

As a global citizen, I support sustainable urban planning, anti-littering campaigns, equitable and eco-friendly manufacturing processes, reforestation, and the likes. That's been my stance my whole life.

However, there were other themes I wanted to explore in my work first: politics, relationships, AI... I just found myself at the right intersection, with the right tools and project, to discuss the state of our planet.

Q: You have this very unique approach to... action scenes? Very complex and always fresh in some

ways. How do you manage to construct such amazing dynamics? Like the Forward Observer in Paris or the skyjacking (wow).

A: Thank you!

I have one main objective when building action scenes or items: **the action must serve the plot**, not the other way around. Action is not just a mechanic employed to thrust the story forward.

It should add further layers to characterization, ambiance, emotional appeal, and messaging. Action is more than a basic process; it is an art form.

Once you understand that as a creative writer, you'll start drafting more exciting scenes that carry higher value for your storytelling.

Q: There's a strong father/daughter dynamic with Malia and Baba/Riz, but sometimes borderline patriarchal. As a father yourself, is there a hidden message there?

A: Fatherhood is arguably one of the most important aspects of my life.

As a writer, any project I take on will, to some extent, be an expression of the soul. I drew inspiration from my own personal experience to depict some of the patterns and behaviors during those father/daughter moments.

But I also wanted to introduce a patriarchal component due to cultural sensibilities and the needs of the story. The more traumatic aspects of their relationship are things I've witnessed but, fortunately, never experienced personally.

Q: It's a spy thriller, in essence. Who are your favorite authors in the genre?

A: I'm an old soul. I used to read John le Carré, Tom Clancy, Robert Ludlum, Vince Flynn, and other staples.

But with this work, in particular, John le Carré was a major influence. I wanted a precise and culturally accurate representation of tradecraft in different settings, and his attention to detail is second to none.

Alex Gansa and his team, who wrote the TV series *Homeland*, were also sources of inspiration. I wanted to create something terrifying, believable, and nuanced in its morality.

Q: What is your position on U.S. foreign policies? I was wondering because I loved the way you painted the reality of war and terrorism.

A: I'm a former U.S. Army service member, but I'm also a student of life. Coming from a diverse household, I've learned to embrace multiple viewpoints at once and sometimes reconcile divergent ideas. I believe in protecting my flesh, my family, my tribe. I believe in standing strong, both physically and mentally.

So, in some form, I think war is sometimes justified—it can even be spiritual.

But I'm also aware that the U.S. has often instrumentalized war to gain access to natural resources, attract foreign investments, and expand its political influence. Terrorism was partly created by the U.S. and its allies.

However, foreign nations also bear responsibility for many dysfunctions within their own territories (Africa, Southeast Asia, the Middle East, etc.). These issues are mostly rooted in unhealed wounds from colonial eras and tribal grudges.

The world is a complex system with shared responsibilities. So is war.

Q: The Night Sisters of Ramza. I'm intrigued. There's magic. Are you planning on a shared universe? Or a spin-off that crosses genres?

A: That sounds exciting! I did initially consider developing a high fantasy novel set after Malia's reset, but I'm reserving magic and fantasy for another project.

Additionally, I wasn't convinced I could effectively shift from a realistic spy thriller to a high fantasy esoteric tale.

Stay tuned for more!

To whoever believed in my calling, thank you.

I silenced the storm *within* and fought an uninvited depression, but in the midst of chaos that was uncalled for, I still found consistent love in writing and storytelling.

As I'm holding onto this anchor, I hope to flourish so I can reach those who share my predicament.

This novel is a love letter to our planet, an ode to the urgency we should display in addressing climate change, which is very real and incurs many damages: financial losses, displacement, the extinction of endangered species, the rising prevalence of cancers at younger ages...

Our inability to shape a global response, one killed early on by competing political agendas and socioeconomics, is the root cause of the very sickness at the core of our Earth and its unsustainable urbanization.

Just like the responses associated with extreme class divide, poverty, late-stage capitalism, and other harmful historical events, only a collective revolt will bear tangible and long-lasting results.

We must grow a shared consciousness that borrows from our individual strengths and act on the basis of a united front.

Take care of the world you live in. We are guests here.

Don't forget to review my titles. **It is instrumental to my success.**

You can find me on The StoryGraph, Amazon, Barnes & Noble, Kobo, Target, Walmart, and all other major retailers.

Plus, I love a good conversation with my readership.

Andre Soares

WHERE TO FIND ME?

Website: https://www.thesoaresprotocol.com/
facebook.com/thesoaresprotocol
instagram.com/thesoaresprotocol

The Forerunner: A Vice Versa Series

C1: A Vice Versa Series

Alidala: A Vice Versa Series

America is a Zoo

Them: A Short Story

The Sunflower Protocol

www.ingramcontent.com/pod-product-compliance
Lightning Source LLC
Chambersburg PA
CBHW032254310726
48973CB00008B/2406